KATHRYN HULICK

WESTON WEI

THE UFO FILES

WIDE EYED EDITIONS

Contents

December 3, 2033

Dear Reader,

For decades, many have suspected that intelligent life might exist on other planets. Some have even searched for evidence of extraterrestrial technology. At long last, we've found it. Or rather, it found us.

Earlier this year, a UFO landed on Earth. The aliens—we call them Visitors—peered across the galaxy and noticed Earth, a single speck of rock amidst a vast sea of other stars and planets. They came here using technology that goes well beyond what humanity has created. These files contain the marvels that we encountered. I am so honored to share our findings with the world.

In the interest of safety and privacy, I have chosen to remain anonymous. You can call me Polaris, the name of the North star, which has always been a guiding light.

I hope I have what it takes to guide humanity at such an important time. A new era in history began the moment the UFO arrived. We have so much still to learn.

Yours truly,

Polaris, Head of Investigations

First Contact

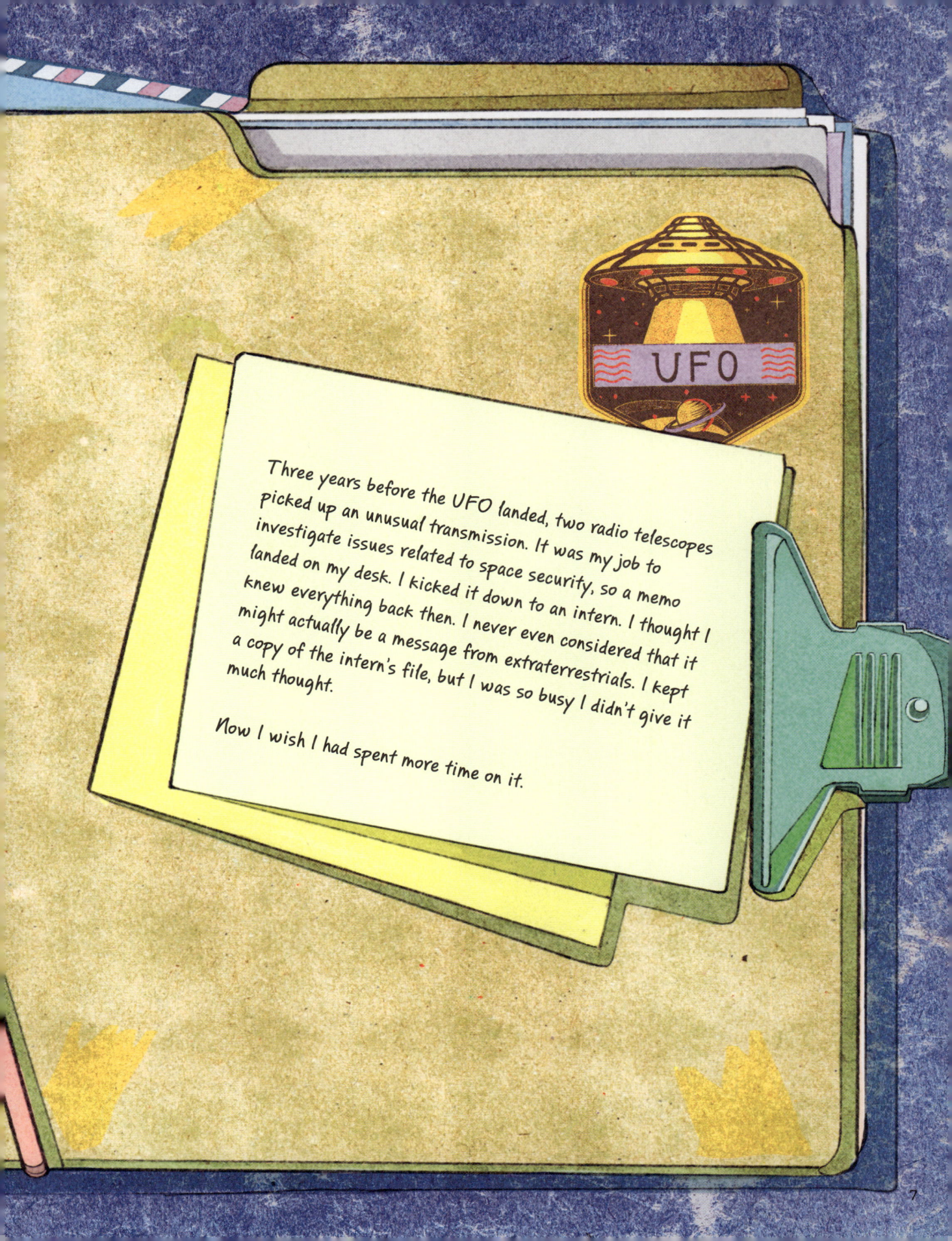

Three years before the UFO landed, two radio telescopes picked up an unusual transmission. It was my job to investigate issues related to space security, so a memo landed on my desk. I kicked it down to an intern. I thought I knew everything back then. I never even considered that it might actually be a message from extraterrestrials. I kept a copy of the intern's file, but I was so busy I didn't give it much thought.

Now I wish I had spent more time on it.

STRANGE SIGNAL FROM SPACE

Could it be aliens?

Are we alone in the universe? Humanity has been asking this question for as long as we have stared up at the night sky. Yesterday, we may have received an answer. Two radio telescopes picked up an unusual signal from space. "It's the best candidate for a technosignature that we've ever received," said Shane Atwood, an astronomer with the SETI Institute in Mountain View, California.

A technosignature is evidence of technology from beyond Earth. And if such technology exists, it stands to reason that alien intelligence built it. But, cautions Atwood, we shouldn't jump to any conclusions just yet.

The signal arrived the morning of Friday, May 24. Cory Torres, a researcher at the Allen Telescope Array in Hat Creek, California, noticed it. First, they had to rule out interference from our own technology, which makes radio noise that can muddy observations. Listening for signals from distant stars is like "trying to hear a faint whisper coming from across the room at a loud, crowded party," says Torres.

The signal came from the general direction of the red dwarf star Ross 128. However, without knowing

Cory Torres at the Allen Telescope Array.
Photograph: Viaan Ranganathan

the amount of power used to send the signal, scientists can't determine how far it traveled. And they have been unable to determine if it might contain a message.

A SETI group in Bologna, Italy, captured the signal, too. "That's never happened before," says Atwood.

However, none of the recordings are very high quality. "The source could be a nearby spy satellite," suggests Atwood. No country or organization has claimed responsibility, though.

Is it a message from extraterrestrials? "We just don't know yet," says Torres.

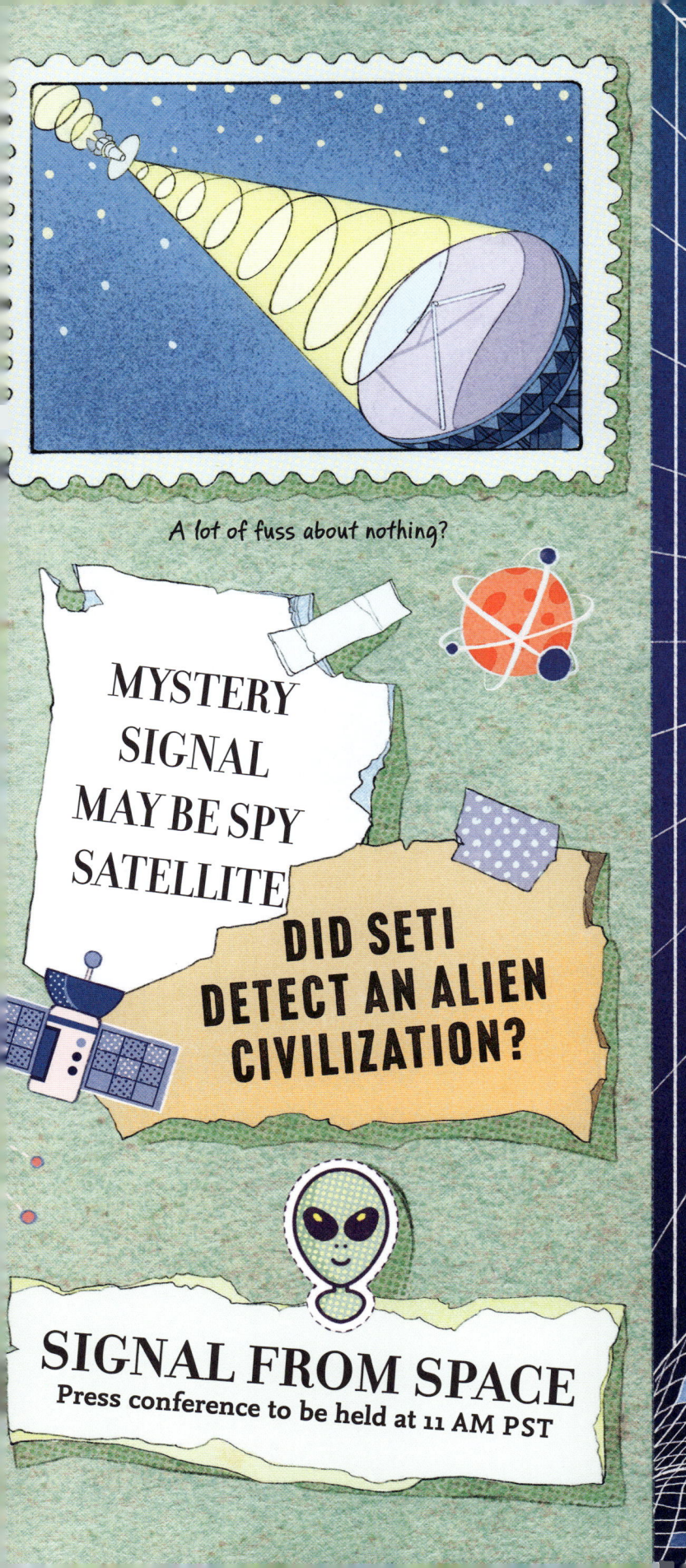

A lot of fuss about nothing?

MYSTERY SIGNAL MAY BE SPY SATELLITE

DID SETI DETECT AN ALIEN CIVILIZATION?

SIGNAL FROM SPACE
Press conference to be held at 11 AM PST

The story of SETI

SETI stands for "the Search for ExtraTerrestrial Intelligence." Many scientists and other experts around the world have participated. In 1984, astronomer Jill Tarter co-founded the SETI Institute.

As of 2024, no scientific evidence of intelligent aliens had been found. But space is huge and we haven't looked everywhere. So, the search carries on. The ongoing Breakthrough Listen Initiative launched in 2015 and is the largest SETI effort in history.

"When I was a small child . . . I was walking along the beach . . . with my dad . . . And I looked up, and I understood that those stars in the sky were like our sun. And it just seemed absolutely natural to me that on a beach, circling one of those stars up there, there would be another creature walking along with its parent by the edge of an ocean and looking up and seeing our sun as a star in their sky."
—Jill Tarter, 2020

A narrow band signal that comes from space could be evidence of alien technology!

Cory: We found something.

Viaan: What?

Cory: A narrow band signal. It was in this morning's observations.

Viaan:

Cory: It's in the hydrogen band.

Viaan: Interesting.

Cory: I'll let you know if we see it again.

Signal captured at Allen Telescope Array

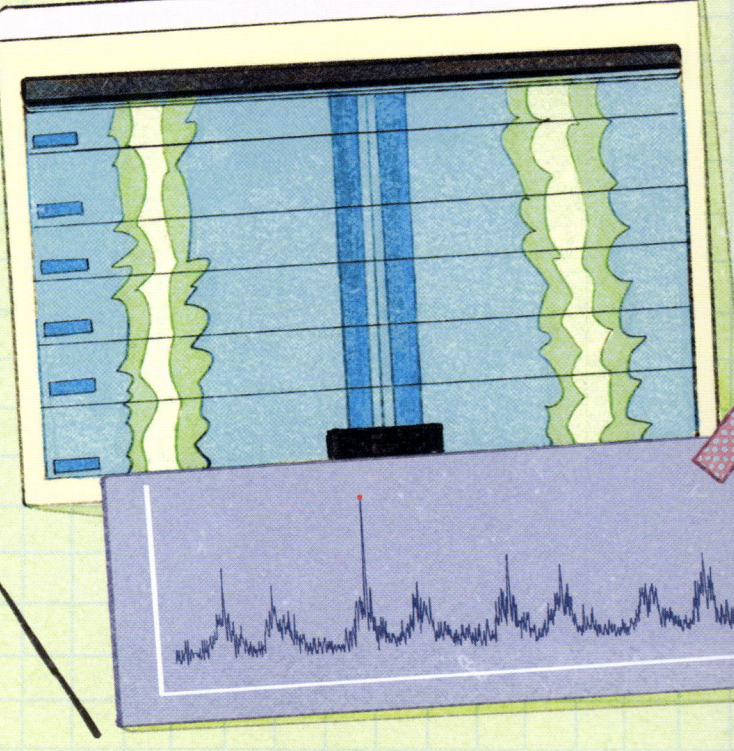

Frequency of the hydrogen band = 1420.4 MHz. Very important for radio astronomy!

Allen Telescope Array, Hat Creek, California, United States

The electromagnetic spectrum

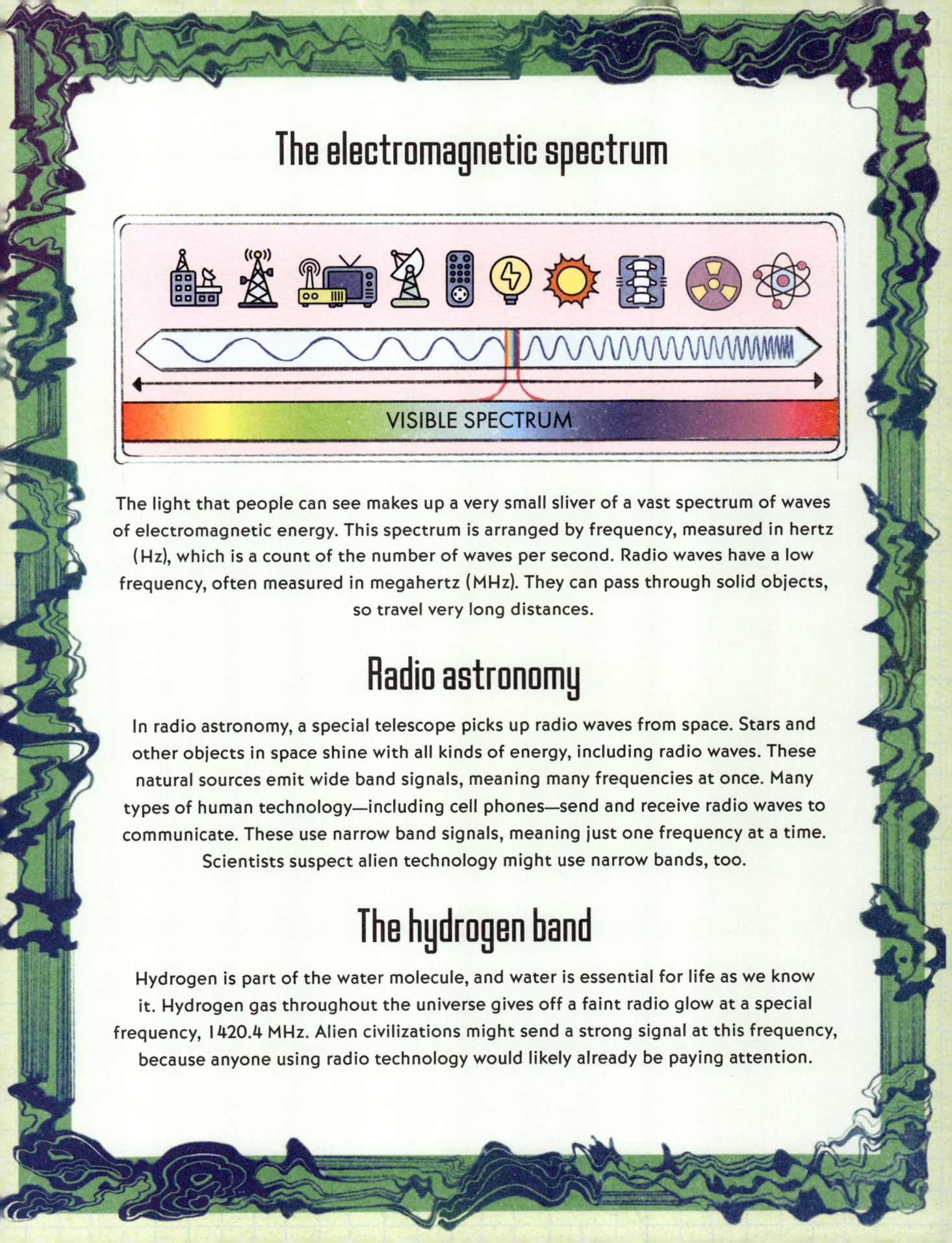

The light that people can see makes up a very small sliver of a vast spectrum of waves of electromagnetic energy. This spectrum is arranged by frequency, measured in hertz (Hz), which is a count of the number of waves per second. Radio waves have a low frequency, often measured in megahertz (MHz). They can pass through solid objects, so travel very long distances.

Radio astronomy

In radio astronomy, a special telescope picks up radio waves from space. Stars and other objects in space shine with all kinds of energy, including radio waves. These natural sources emit wide band signals, meaning many frequencies at once. Many types of human technology—including cell phones—send and receive radio waves to communicate. These use narrow band signals, meaning just one frequency at a time. Scientists suspect alien technology might use narrow bands, too.

The hydrogen band

Hydrogen is part of the water molecule, and water is essential for life as we know it. Hydrogen gas throughout the universe gives off a faint radio glow at a special frequency, 1420.4 MHz. Alien civilizations might send a strong signal at this frequency, because anyone using radio technology would likely already be paying attention.

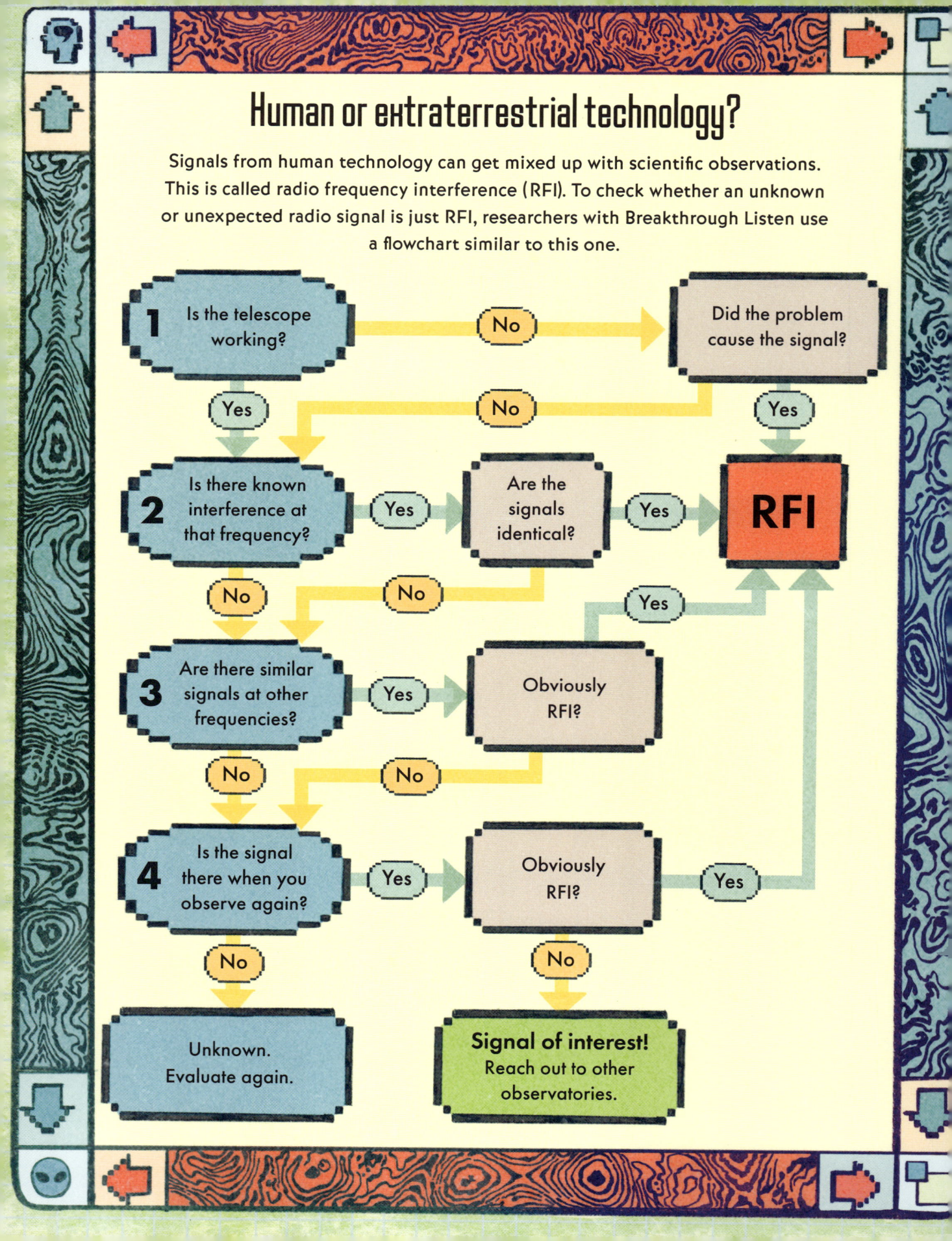

Human or extraterrestrial technology?

Signals from human technology can get mixed up with scientific observations. This is called radio frequency interference (RFI). To check whether an unknown or unexpected radio signal is just RFI, researchers with Breakthrough Listen use a flowchart similar to this one.

1 Is the telescope working? — No → Did the problem cause the signal?

Yes ↓   Did the problem cause the signal? — Yes ↓ → **RFI**

2 Is there known interference at that frequency? — Yes → Are the signals identical? — Yes → **RFI**

No ↓   Are the signals identical? — No ↓

3 Are there similar signals at other frequencies? — Yes → Obviously RFI? — Yes → **RFI**

No ↓   Obviously RFI? — No ↓

4 Is the signal there when you observe again? — Yes → Obviously RFI? — Yes → **RFI**

No ↓   Obviously RFI? — No ↓

Unknown. Evaluate again.

Signal of interest! Reach out to other observatories.

International Press Conference, May 24, 2030.
Medicina Radio Astronomical Station, Italy

These side bands contain the signal's information.

This is the carrier signal. It adds power to help the information reach farther.

To: Medicina Radio Astronomical Station;
Green Bank Observatory; Parkes Observatory
CC: SETI team
Subject: Narrow band signal of interest

May 24, 2030, 8:35 AM

We found an interesting signal this morning and haven't found any obvious interference. I'm attaching the data. Could we have director approval for telescope time today?

Best,
Viaan Ran
Allen Tele

To: Viaan Ranganathan
Subject: RE: Narrow band signal of interest

May 24, 2030, 9:21 AM

We found a record in our data from earlier today of the same signal!!! Can you call us now? We'll need to hold a press conference as soon as possible.

Best,
Arabella Moretti
Medicina Radio Astronomical Station

To: SETI team
Subject: RE: RE: Narrow band signal of interest

May 27, 2030, 1:12 PM

The data for Green Bank ID# GBT28A-024 came in. We have not detected the signal of interest again. At this point, the source remains unknown. We recommend coming up with a schedule for repeat observations.

Sincerely,
Viaan Ranganathan
Allen Telescope Array

#FreeET has been trending. Some claim the government is hiding information about the signal. HA! I'm the government. I know just as much as they do!

Experiencer2019:

If we fear the extraterrestrials, we are not yet ready to meet them. #FreeET

MMainon1:

What if they're coming to colonize Earth?

Ayanna_knows:

Any civilization advanced enough to visit would have evolved beyond the horrors of European colonization. I welcome them with open arms. I hope they bring answers. #FreeET

AdamSingFa:

You guys, this is all a ruse. The government is distracting us from their spy satellites with this fake alien thing.

Talk-show appearance with SETI director Shane Atwood, June 1, 2030.

HOST: That mystery signal got the whole world's attention. Some say you have information you're not sharing.

SHANE: The data files that the telescopes captured are freely available for anyone to download.

HOST: Is there a message hidden in it?

SHANE: No one has been able to find one—the data quality isn't great.

HOST: Did intelligent aliens send it?

SHANE: We don't know yet. That's the beauty of science. We don't always have the answers, but we do the hard work to find them. At SETI, anything we discover, we will share.

Where is everybody?

Our Milky Way galaxy contains around 100 billion stars, and lots of them host planets. So why haven't we heard from alien life forms? In 1961, astronomer Frank Drake came up with a way to answer the question using math.

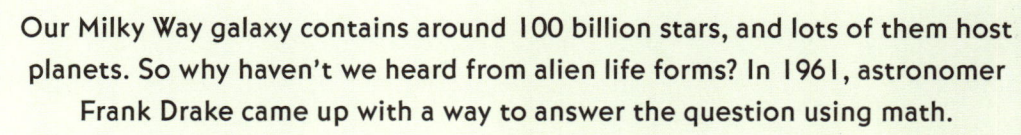

$$N = R_* \times f_p \times n_e \times f_l \times f_i \times f_c \times L$$

It's not as complicated as it looks!

N = The number of civilizations sending signals that we could detect right now

R_* = The number of new stars that form per year

f_p = The portion of stars that have planets

n_e = The number of planets per star with conditions for life

f_l = The portion of these planets where life actually appears

f_i = The portion of those planets where intelligent life evolves

f_c = The portion of civilizations that send signals that could reach Earth

L = The average number of years that these civilizations send out signals

Scientists don't know what numbers to plug into most parts of the equation. Many planets are difficult places for life to survive. On Earth, humans are the only species to ever send signals into space. And we've only been doing this for one hundred years. That's less than the blink of an eye compared to the 4.5 billion years Earth has existed!

Any alien civilizations likely rise and fall long before or after us, or are too far away to reach us with signals. But contact is still possible.

The Spaceship

As the next few years passed, I must admit I forgot all about that mysterious signal. At work, I rose through the ranks. When we heard that a handful of people had seen or recorded a very unusual object falling from space, I put together a team and traveled out to the middle of nowhere. Never in a million years could I have imagined what we'd discover out there.

From: MeteorWatch moderators
To: NASA Center for Near Earth Object Studies; SETI Institute
May 22, 2033 at 9:05 AM
Subject: Unknown object sighted by multiple observers

Dear NASA and SETI,

We'd like to bring your attention to an unusual event. At around 1:10 AM, several members in our community of experienced meteor-watchers tracked a large, unidentified object. From multiple observations in southern California, Arizona, and New Mexico, we have determined that the object entered the atmosphere at around 27,000 miles per hour, and at a very shallow angle. The absence of a long tail indicates it did not break up. It seems to have landed in the Chihuahuan Desert. All our observation data is available online.

This object was not in any catalog of near-Earth objects. It was probably a large metal meteorite. But, as unbelievable as this sounds, some members of our community suggest it may have been an alien spacecraft. They plan to search where it must have landed.

Thank you,

MeteorWatch moderators

This was a sonic boom, caused by the object going faster than the speed of sound when it hit the atmosphere.

Mariana Sanchez of California shot this video from a passenger airplane
on May 22, 2033, 1:15 AM

I interviewed several eyewitnesses. Teens Kai M. and Sylvie E. were out in the desert that night and had a clear view of the light.

Polaris: Can you describe the light you saw?

Kai: It was epic. It streaked across the sky for at least a minute.

Sylvie: It was brighter than the stars at first but if you weren't looking you'd probably miss it.

Kai: Was it a shooting star?

Polaris: We're still investigating. Anything else?

Sylvie: We heard a sound, almost like thunder.

Kai: That was a couple minutes later.

Sylvie: It was weird because there wasn't any bad weather or anything.

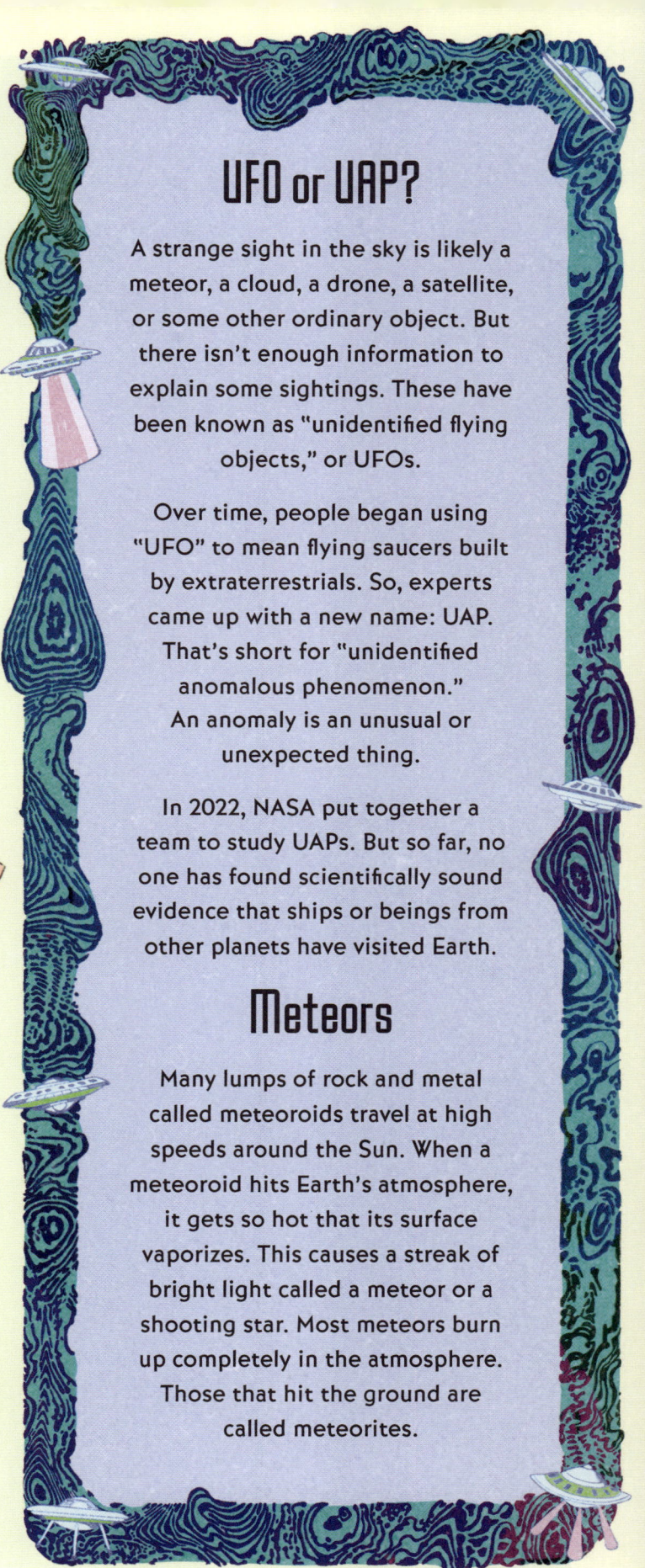

UFO or UAP?

A strange sight in the sky is likely a meteor, a cloud, a drone, a satellite, or some other ordinary object. But there isn't enough information to explain some sightings. These have been known as "unidentified flying objects," or UFOs.

Over time, people began using "UFO" to mean flying saucers built by extraterrestrials. So, experts came up with a new name: UAP. That's short for "unidentified anomalous phenomenon." An anomaly is an unusual or unexpected thing.

In 2022, NASA put together a team to study UAPs. But so far, no one has found scientifically sound evidence that ships or beings from other planets have visited Earth.

Meteors

Many lumps of rock and metal called meteoroids travel at high speeds around the Sun. When a meteoroid hits Earth's atmosphere, it gets so hot that its surface vaporizes. This causes a streak of bright light called a meteor or a shooting star. Most meteors burn up completely in the atmosphere. Those that hit the ground are called meteorites.

May 24, 2033, 3:18 PM

Several teams searched the desert for a meteorite crater and found nothing. So I joined a group of SETI scientists who had calculated what path the object would have taken if it had somehow slowed down while landing. That led us right to it.

In awe, I walked close enough to take this photo. Within an hour, the military had arrived. The General was so jumpy I nicknamed him "Jackrabbit." He made everyone leave and swiftly set up a perimeter. Thankfully, my security clearance allowed me inside.

BREAKING: Unidentified Object from Space Under Investigation

Dr. Jayne Stafford, NASA: We are here to confirm reports that an object from space has landed in the United States. This anomaly is technological and not natural. However, we do not yet know its purpose or origin. We ask that civilians and members of the media practice patience and caution as we proceed with our investigation.

Jackrabbit: For public safety, we are not allowing access to the landing site.

Shane Atwood, SETI Institute: We will now take a few questions.

Q: Is it really a UFO? From another planet?

Atwood: We don't have enough information yet. However, it does not resemble any known Earth technology.

Q: Did any aliens emerge? Are you hiding them somewhere?

Dr. Stafford: Nothing has come out of the object. It experienced at least 30 Gs during its descent. The likelihood that anything is alive in there is slim to zero.

Atwood: You know everything we know. This will be an open, collaborative, international investigation. The United Nations is establishing an Anomaly Committee to oversee everything.

Q: This is the first evidence of extraterrestrial life! How does that make you feel?

Atwood: We don't yet know the object's origin or purpose. But we are very excited to begin our research!

That's me! I was completely overwhelmed . . .

And that's Jackrabbit. He fidgeted the whole time.

Riding a roller coaster

When you rapidly speed up or slow down while riding on a roller coaster, you experience changing G-forces. The "G" stands for gravity. The force of gravity at Earth's surface is one G. Lower Gs make you feel like you're floating or flying. Higher Gs press you into your seat. People can survive brief moments of G-forces over nine G, but the higher these forces are and the longer they last, the deadlier they get.

Safety and Security Report, May 25, 2033.

Perimeter and base camp established. Scans for explosives and toxic chemicals all negative. Radiation level normal. The object and all nearby debris have remained motionless and unchanged throughout operations. The object may be broken or nonfunctional.

Military robots deployed observation equipment. Complete list of equipment and readings available upon request. All personnel must continue to remain at least half a mile away from the object.

Let's Go, Team UFO!

United Nations Anomaly Committee (UNAC) = The Big Boss

Jackrabbit = Head of Safety and Security (his team: soldiers, doctors, emergency response experts, etc.)

Polaris = Head of Investigations (my team: scientists and researchers)

Jayne Stafford
NASA. Coding, robotics.

Shane Atwood
SETI astronomer.
Policy and ethics.

Ayan Banerjee
Engineer and physicist. Materials.

Carmen Cardoso
Engineer.
Rocket scientist.

Nora Willis
Astrobiologist.
Microbes, life forms.

UFO Materials New to Science!

May 27, 2033

If you didn't already believe that the UFO came from another planet, now you will. It's made of materials new to science. "They are astonishing," said Ayan Banerjee, a physicist and engineer with the Indian Space Research Organization who is part of the anomaly investigation. "One material alters in structure as temperature and pressure change. It's like it can shape-shift to maintain strength under extreme conditions."

Robots brought back samples of debris from near the UFO yesterday. Several teams of engineers worked through the night to analyze them. Spectroscopy revealed that the materials contained fairly ordinary metals and organic molecules.

Next, these engineers used X-ray diffraction and scanning-tunneling microscopes to look at the structure of the materials, meaning how their atoms and molecules are arranged. A material's structure gives it many of its important properties, such as heat resistance or flexibility.

This is when the surprises began. At the nanoscale, these materials have complex and beautiful structures. "I don't think any lab on Earth could have created this material," says Banerjee.

<u>Watch the livestream of the retrieval here!</u>

 kylie8910: Destroy #UFO33 now, before it's too late.

 himom3789991: Where are you hiding the aliens?

 OneSkye: Amazing! This is Earth's moment to shine. Science rules!

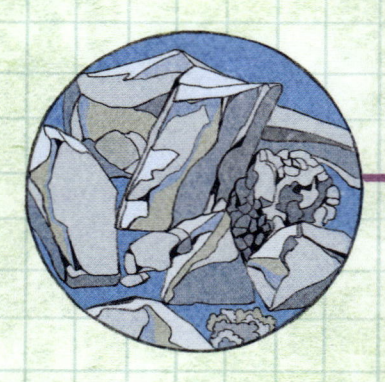

Material A:
silvery metallic plating

Material B:
a flexible cord

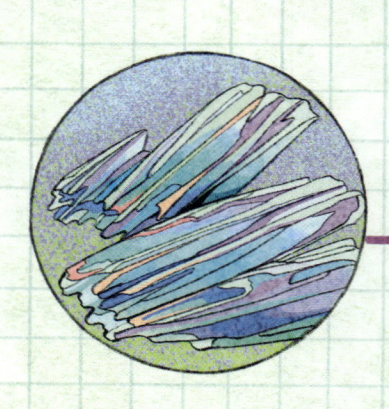

Material C:
a shimmery plastic

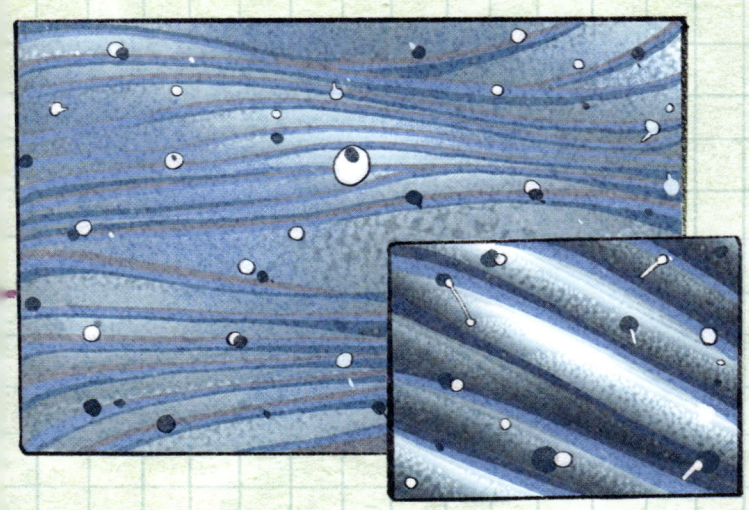

Contains threads of carbon, aluminum, tungsten, hafnium, and silicon. This material is lightweight, tough, and flexible. Particles distributed throughout help resist heat and radiation damage. May have shielded the object in space and in Earth's atmosphere.

Carbon nanotubes. Similar to known materials, but stronger and lighter.

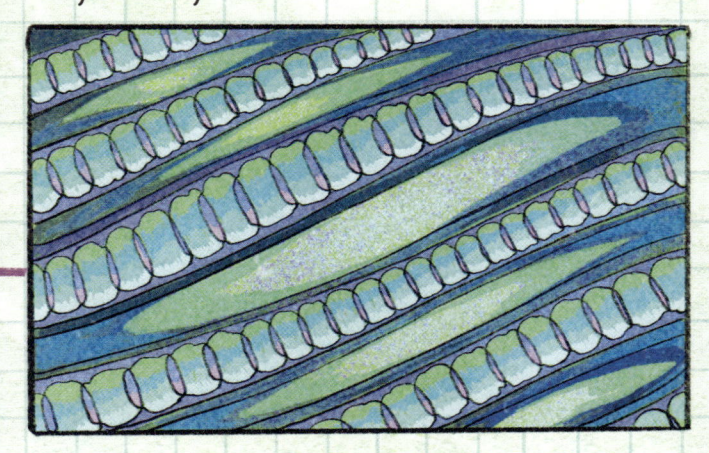

Organic, yet magnetic. A very thin film with structures that may alter the color of light.

The elements

Everything in the universe is made of different types of atoms, called elements. A molecule is a group of atoms stuck together. Carbon is an element that shows up in all organic molecules, including body parts, plants, and plastics. Ceramics and metals are examples of inorganic materials.

Detecting atoms

Spectroscopy reveals the kinds of elements that make up a material. To determine structure, researchers use different techniques. X-ray diffraction shines X-rays through a material to reveal how molecules inside are arranged. Scanning-tunneling microscopes detect the pattern of atoms in a surface.

Nanotechnology

Building or changing structures at the scale of atoms and molecules is called nanotechnology. Engineers use nanotechnology to create new kinds of medicines, electronics, and advanced materials.

May 30, 2033

Dear team,

Happy Memorial Day! I have important news to share. About fifteen minutes ago, a red-tailed hawk landed on top of the UFO. (Everyone in the world now calls it a UFO, so I will, too).

Then a door opened. Four flying things—I'm calling them BugBots—rose up from inside. Startled, the bird flew off and the BugBots retreated. Most of us had assumed this was some sort of broken relic. Now we know that it is functional.

Some members of the Safety and Security team see this incident as a threat. But I disagree. The bird was not harmed, and none of our equipment has been damaged, either.

We have plenty of evidence that the UFO is not a weapon. It is a visitor. And it may be trying to communicate. I am putting together a proposal for the UN committee that outlines a plan for next steps. Now is a time for scientific curiosity, diverse perspectives, and open minds.

Sincerely,

Polaris

We asked the public what might make the BugBots emerge again. People around the world bombarded us with millions of ideas. Volunteers sorted and translated everything. Many people said we should force our way inside. A few even wanted to destroy the UFO. But we opted for restraint and respect. We tried a few of the most interesting ideas.

May 31, 2033, 7:05 PM. A drone recreates the hawk's landing. No response.

June 1, 2033, 3:14 PM. Sgt. Toby Brown approaches the anomaly. No response.

June 2, 2033, 9:31 AM. Offered gifts and scents. No response.

June 2, 2033, 1:15 PM. Sent another hawk. No response.

June 3, 2033, 10:00 PM. Nocturnal approach. Success!

What if the aliens are nocturnal? It was almost dark when the hawk landed.

—Njeri Chege, age 15, Kenya

Finally, we approached the UFO again, but this time at night. We turned off all our lights. As we stood there in the darkness, something remarkable began to happen . . .

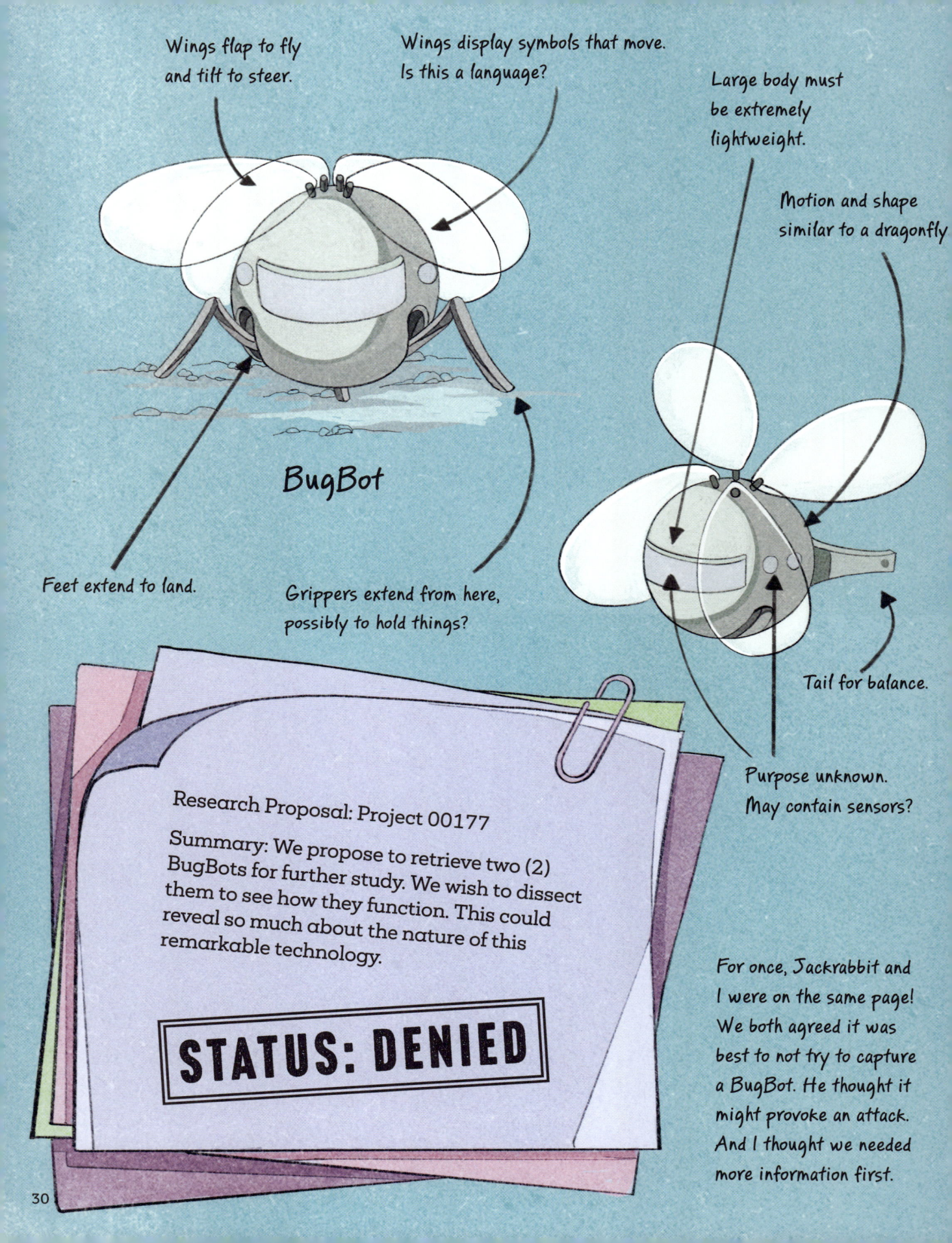

BugBot Observation, June 4-5, 2033

Team leader: Polaris

Engineer: Carmen Cardoso

Astrobiologist: Nora Willis

Polaris: 8:05 PM. We are setting up low-light video cameras and <u>EMF meters</u>.

This tool detects electromagnetic energy from wiring, electrical equipment, magnetic fields, and more.

Nora: 8:19 PM. We turned off all artificial lights. Recording has started.

Carmen: The BugBots immediately started the show! The EMF meter picked up signals. These are indeed robots.

Nora: 10:11 PM. Base camp is receiving a radio transmission from the UFO.

Polaris: 11:11 PM. The radio transmission has been repeating for one hour.

[Loud crashing sound]

Nora: 11:28 PM. A team member (you know who you are) accidentally knocked over a light pole in the dark. The BugBots retreated while displaying what we are calling "panic lights."

Polaris: 1:15 AM. We're returning to base camp.

Drones

A drone is any aircraft that flies without a pilot on board. Some drones are so small they fit in the palm of a hand. Usually, a person on the ground flies a drone using a controller. But autonomous drones fly themselves. Engineers have created very tiny drones inspired by insects. Most of these little bots have a tether that acts as a power cord since they are too small to carry the weight of a battery. Engineers have also used magnets to control and power tiny robots.

The dragonfly

This common insect is a master of flight. A dragonfly has four wings that flap. Each wing can independently speed up, slow down, or even swivel to different angles.

The Language

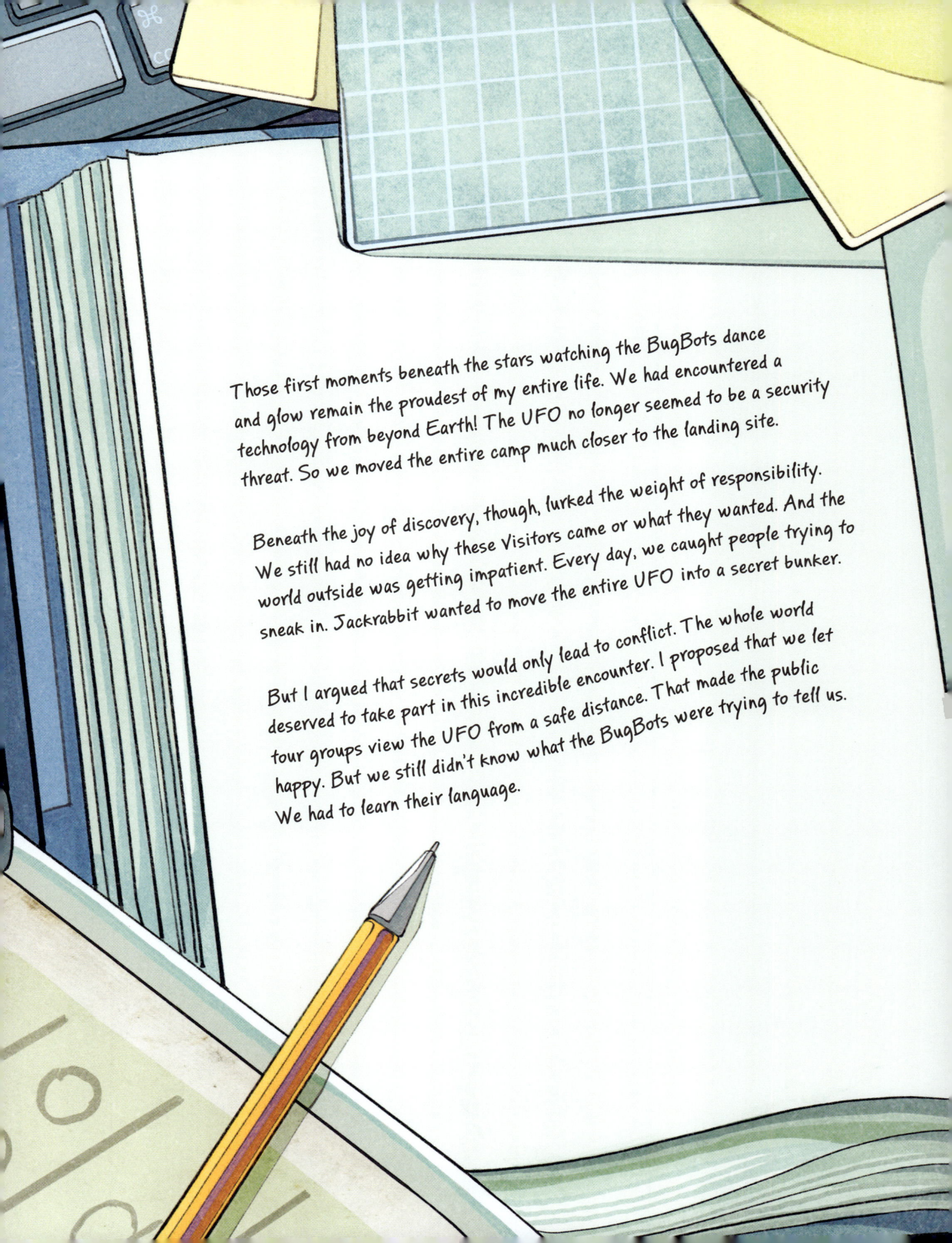

Those first moments beneath the stars watching the BugBots dance and glow remain the proudest of my entire life. We had encountered a technology from beyond Earth! The UFO no longer seemed to be a security threat. So we moved the entire camp much closer to the landing site.

Beneath the joy of discovery, though, lurked the weight of responsibility. We still had no idea why these Visitors came or what they wanted. And the world outside was getting impatient. Every day, we caught people trying to sneak in. Jackrabbit wanted to move the entire UFO into a secret bunker.

But I argued that secrets would only lead to conflict. The whole world deserved to take part in this incredible encounter. I proposed that we let tour groups view the UFO from a safe distance. That made the public happy. But we still didn't know what the BugBots were trying to tell us. We had to learn their language.

My team appeared on radio and TV shows to share our findings.

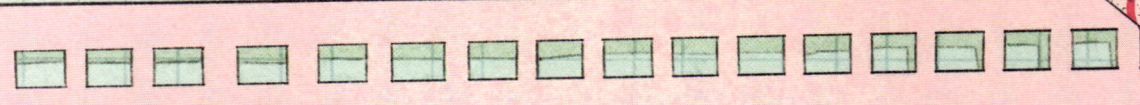

Radio transcript, June 4, 2033

Host: That UFO light show was incredible! Why did the aliens wait so long to do this?

Shane Atwood: We prefer the term "Visitors," because "aliens" might imply that they don't belong or aren't welcome. Anyway, all our early observations took place during daylight or with artificial lights. The Visitors must have been waiting for darkness.

Jayne Stafford: I also want to mention the radio transmission. It may not be as impressive as the lights, but the Visitors sent it at the same time.

Host: What does it all mean?

Shane: That's what we're trying to find out. If this is a message, we'd love to decode it. Our team has linguists and computer scientists working on it, but we've also put all the files online so anyone can help.

Host: This is such a great idea. If you're an engineer, coder, artist, anything—go to "The Visitors Forum" and join the effort.

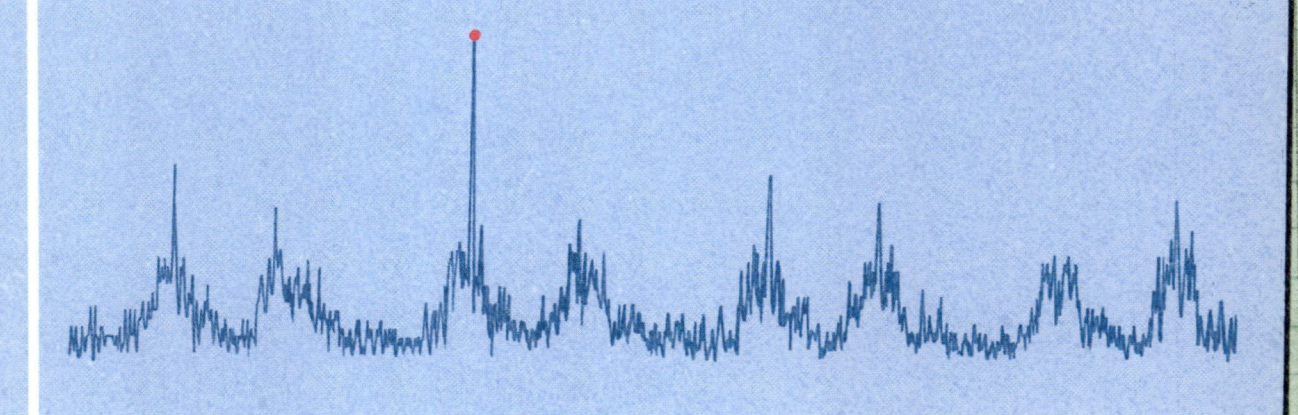

The Visitors' radio signal

Power [dB]

Frequency [MHz]

The transmission from the UFO matches the one from space that SETI picked up three years ago! The Visitors told us they were coming.

Visitors Forum: Update

Shane Atwood [Policy and Ethics]: We've extracted data from the radio transmission. But all we can find in it so far is noise. When we play the radio signal back at the UFO, it does not respond. Maybe the BugBots' light displays and the radio message are two ways of saying the same thing, or one holds the key to interpreting the other. Please share your ideas.

Tatsuya: I found a way to interpret the data visually, but it just looks like noisy blobs. Are we even on the right track?

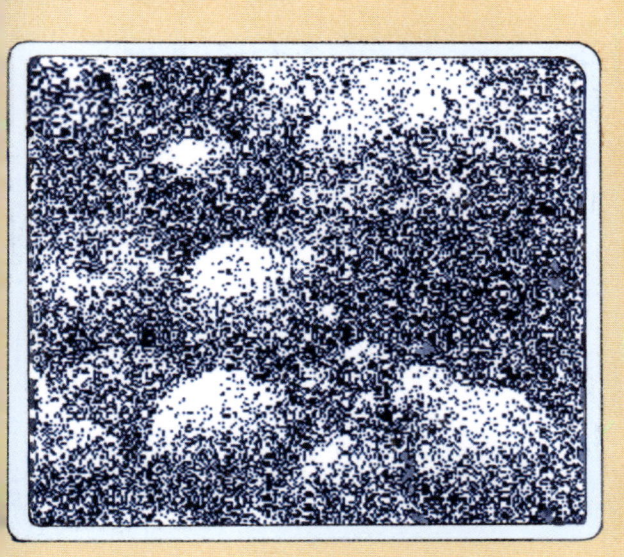

mario.elf: In order to build a spaceship, you have to understand basic math and science. We should start there.

Tatsuya: The message could just be art or space graffiti.

Luna6077: Could it be a star map? Or maybe the blobs represent atoms or molecules?

YvanBoucher: The BugBot light show reminds me of sign languages.

A Sign in Space

If Earth ever receives a message from an extraterrestrial civilization, will we have any hope of decoding it? "A Sign in Space" is an art project that explores this question. Artist Daniela De Paulis created a cryptic message. With the help of SETI scientists, she encoded it into a radio signal. In May 2023, an ESA spacecraft orbiting Mars transmitted the message. Four radio astronomy observatories on Earth picked it up.

Volunteers around the world managed to extract data from the signal. But it was extremely difficult to decipher its meaning. Over a year later, a father-daughter team finally succeeded! They discovered these shapes, which represent different amino acids. These are some of the basic building blocks of all life on Earth.

Visitors Forum: Why are the Visitors Here? I Wish I Could Tell You

Yasmine Crane [Linguistics]: What's inside the UFO? Why did it come here? Many of you don't understand why we haven't just asked the Visitors directly. I thought I'd take a moment to explain.

I'm a xenolinguist—that's a language expert who tries to imagine what contact with extraterrestrials might be like. I am thrilled to be joining the UFO investigation team. Our goal is to talk with the Visitors, but this won't be easy.

In all spoken human languages, words carry meaning. Sounds called phonemes mark the difference between words. For example, the sounds "d" and "l" mark the difference between "dog" and "log." But you can say "dog" loudly or quietly and it's still the same word.

The symbols that the BugBots display could be a language. But where are the words? Are they in the shapes? The brightness? The movement? The radio message is a mystery, too.

When two people who speak different languages try to communicate, they can point, make faces, and act out things that the other person will understand. This may not work with the BugBots. They seem to be robots and they don't have bodies like ours. They may not even realize that our words and gestures are attempts to communicate.

In summary, this will be the most exciting and daunting challenge Earth's linguists have ever faced! Hopefully, we'll find answers to all your questions.

The UFO landing impacted people in many different ways. Allowing tour groups to view the UFO really drove this home. A member of our team tacked this list to the wall. Soon, we were all using these nicknames for the people who came to visit. It helped relieve the stress of the constant attention our work received.

The Cosmic Call

In 1960, Hans Freudenthal created the first language designed for communication with extraterrestrials. He called it LINCOS. In 1999 and 2003, researchers used this language in two broadcasts called The Cosmic Call. The first Cosmic Call used repeated pulses for numbers, then introduced a symbol for each number. From there, math equations introduced new symbols. The idea was that any civilization with advanced technology should recognize basic math.

When the first signal in the Cosmic Call gets decoded correctly, this is part of the result. This shows the numbers 0 through 9 as a series of dots, then as binary code, and finally as a symbol. ≢ represents an equals sign.

1) **Partyer**—Super excited about being part of this moment in history. Celebrates with dancing, music, costumes, and more.

2) **Prepper**—Worried or angry about the UFO. Prepares for an attack or confrontation.

3) **Prayer**—Sees the UFO as a religious sign or magical entity. Seeks answers or healing.

4) **Puzzler**—Curious about the UFO. Wants to understand why it is here and how it works.

5) **Paparazzi**—Looking to make money off the UFO through mementos, images, and news.

Research Proposal: Project 00233

Summary: We propose using artificial intelligence (AI) to analyze BugBot light displays.

Details: The AI model we plan to use is called a generative adversarial network (GAN). One half, called the discriminator, uses machine learning to go through examples of real BugBot displays until it can recognize them. The other half, called the generator, will invent its own visual displays. It will learn to fool the discriminator into thinking these are real. Finally, we will study the system to find out what it takes to create a display that seems like a real one. This will reveal what parts of a BugBot display may carry meaning.

Status: APPROVED

Comment: Congratulations! Teams from around the world are submitting thousands of proposals. Yours has been selected. You have been approved to record on the night of June 7–8, 2033.

The BugBots only came out at night when people (or animals) were nearby. They wouldn't respond to our robots. So we became nocturnal ourselves, staying up all night to record the displays.

Machine learning

Artificial intelligence (AI) is any technology that makes a machine behave in a smart way. Machine learning is a popular type of AI. During the learning process, an AI model makes guesses and checks if they are right or wrong. Then it shifts its own programming to make mistakes less likely and successes more likely. Machine learning has helped train computers and robots to translate languages as well as discover potential new medicines, generate text and images, and much more.

Report: Project 00233

Update: The GAN worked beautifully. The BugBot displays seem similar to human sign languages. They contain moving and changing symbols which we are calling visual phonemes.

BugBot Visual Phonemes:

- Type of shape: spiral, circle, curving lines, dots

- Shape movements: expanding, shrinking, fading, blinking, moving up or down

- Color does not seem important

This chart reveals how the GAN found one visual phoneme, an expanding circle:

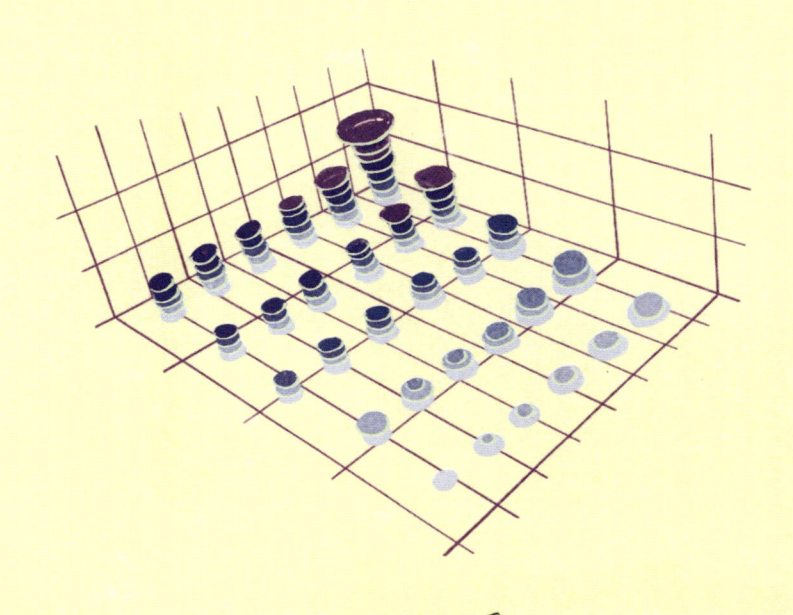

Project CETI

Sperm whales click at each other in exchanges that seem like conversations. Project CETI (Cetacean Translation Initiative) is recording these whales and using AI to try to translate their clicks. Cetacean is the scientific term for a whale, but the name is also a play on SETI, since the researchers see whales as an otherworldly intelligence that we should try to better understand.

Team Meeting, June 8, 2033

Yasmine: We're here to talk about field linguistics. This usually involves interacting with people in order to learn their language. BugBots, of course, aren't human. So what do we need to consider before we begin?

Polaris: The BugBots are electronic. But they might have a sense of self or personhood that we need to respect.

Jackrabbit: Even if they're mindless robots, someone else may be monitoring everything that happens here.

Yasmine: Either way, we have no way of knowing what sort of culture these BugBots come from. An action that seems completely normal to us might offend, anger, or scare them.

Jackrabbit: The Safety and Security team will be ready to neutralize any threat.

Polaris: I'm sure that won't be necessary.

Jayne: Let's stay on topic, please. My team is setting up equipment so we can play BugBot recordings back to them in real time.

Shane: Can they hear and see us?

Nora: We know they react to loud noises, but we have no evidence that they hear or react to speech. They also know when we are near the ship, even in the dark. So they probably detect infrared light.

Carmen: We should make ourselves and our language more visible to them.

Polaris: I'll ask The Visitors Forum for ideas.

Jayne: Great. The first exchange will be the night of June 12–13.

What's infrared?

Infrared is a type of light. We can't see it, but we can feel it as heat. Some animals see infrared light. Even in the dark, a snake can sense a mouse's body heat. Night-vision goggles give people this ability. They convert infrared light into a visible glow.

Visitors Forum: Light Language App

Yoonicorn12345: Hi Visitors Forum! My sister and I made an app. As you talk, it uses AI to turn your speech into glowing text. The BugBots use a visual language, so this is a way to show them our language.—Ha-yoon (14) and Ji-ah (12), South Korea

Visitors Forum: Glow Suit Concept

DenzDrawz: This suit makes actions and gestures more obvious in the dark. Hope y'all like it!—Denzel Edwards, costume designer

On June 11, Denzel Edwards and the young app developers joined our team for a test run of all the gear.

Our supplies for the first BugBot language exchange.

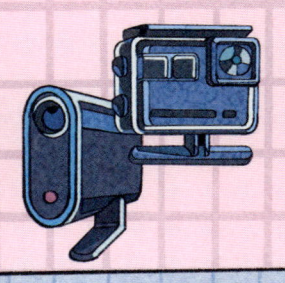

June 13–14, 2033. The BugBot Exchanges, Night 01

Introductions

9:00–9:22 PM: Yasmine Crane, Carmen Cardoso, and Henrik Jacobsen approach the UFO and set up their equipment. They are wearing glowsuits. They each have a tablet that can display glowing letters or play back the Light Language. The BugBots emerge and begin to display light patterns.

9:24–9:30 PM: We begin by labeling ourselves and the BugBots.

9:30–9:35 PM: The BugBots respond. They use a spiral symbol to identify themselves. We are making rapid progress!

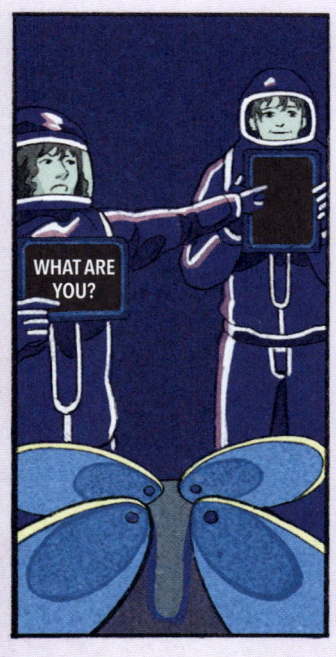

Counting

9:35–9:51 PM: We demonstrate counting. The BugBots don't seem to understand.

   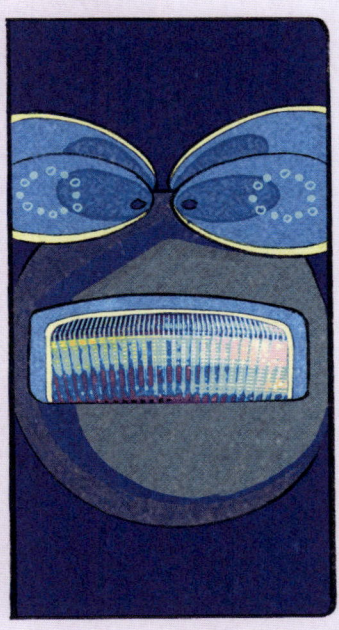

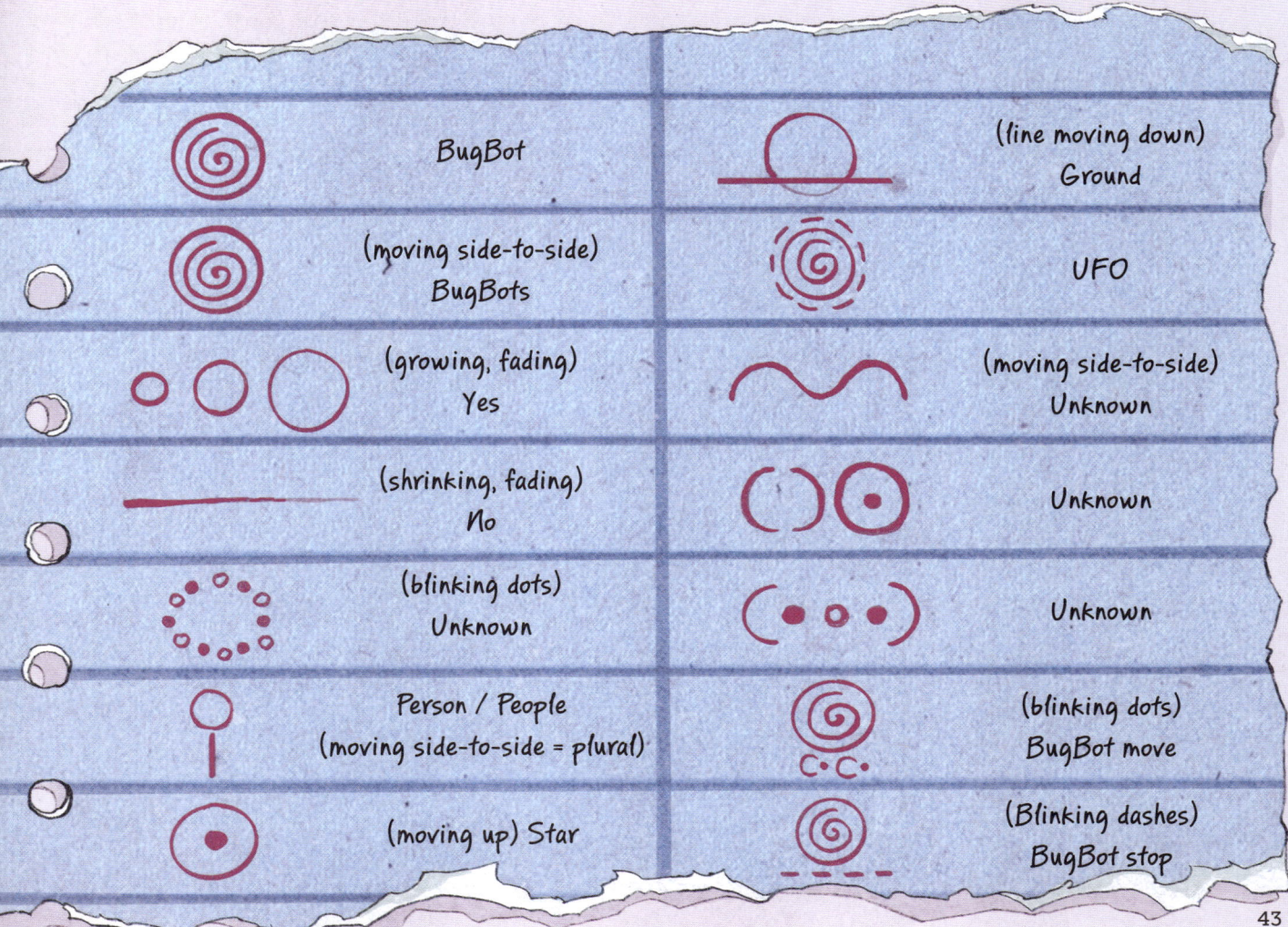

BugBot		(line moving down) Ground	
(moving side-to-side) BugBots		UFO	
(growing, fading) Yes		(moving side-to-side) Unknown	
(shrinking, fading) No		Unknown	
(blinking dots) Unknown		Unknown	
Person / People (moving side-to-side = plural)		(blinking dots) BugBot move	
(moving up) Star		(Blinking dashes) BugBot stop	

The complete records of nightly exchanges would fill another book the size of this one! These are some of the most interesting ones. It takes a very long time to piece together an unknown language. So we used very simple words and phrases. Linguists here at camp and around the world worked at deciphering the Light Language. The original BugBot display seemed to be some sort of greeting. They were trying to talk to us. Then one night, they displayed English words. They'd learned our language!

June 17–18, 2033. The BugBot Exchanges, Night 05

June 23–24, 2033. The BugBot Exchanges, Night 11

9:23–11:51 PM We try many different ways of asking the BugBots why they came to Earth and what they want. They don't reply or say they don't understand.

12:03 AM We play the radio message that the UFO sent out. We ask what it is.

Visitors Forum: General Discussion

YvanBoucher: I've spent countless hours trying to decode this radio signal, and it just means "hello?"

mario.elf: So I think this is what happened. They noticed Earth using radio. So they made a radio signal that they thought was just like ours.

YvanBoucher: Like how a hunter makes a duck call?

OneSkye: I sure hope they're not hunters, lol.

mario.elf: Biologists copy animal sounds in their research sometimes.

YvanBoucher: So they're studying us maybe.

July 8–9, 2033. The BugBot Exchanges, Night 26

2:07–2:23 AM We demonstrate drinking and eating.
The BugBots react strangely.

This was the first time we'd done any eating or drinking in front of the BugBots. The water got them very excited but eating caused them to start flashing their panic lights. It seemed to terrify them.

Team Meeting, July 9, 7:05 AM

Jackrabbit: This meeting is a waste of time. I should be preparing my forces in case of attack!

Polaris: If we do that, the BugBots might get even more upset. All they did was fly away and hide.

Yasmine: Misunderstandings happen whenever different cultures meet. How can we convince them we meant no harm?

Polaris: We don't have the words to express feeling sorry. We don't even know if apologies are part of their culture. But we can promise not to eat in front of them again.

Nora: They liked the water. Maybe bring them more of that?

Jackrabbit: You have two weeks. Then I'm shutting this whole exchange thing down.

We waited for hours every night beside the UFO with bottled water, holding tablets saying: PERSONS GIVE WATER. NO EAT. At midnight, we'd leave the water behind and return to camp. On our last night, the BugBots finally appeared. To our surprise, they invited us inside.

What is culture?

Human cultures are groups of people who share beliefs, values, traditions, and customs. They may also have their own language, music, art, and institutions. The culture or cultures you grow up with impact how you see the world. Often, something that seems normal or good in one culture may surprise people from a different culture.

The Technology

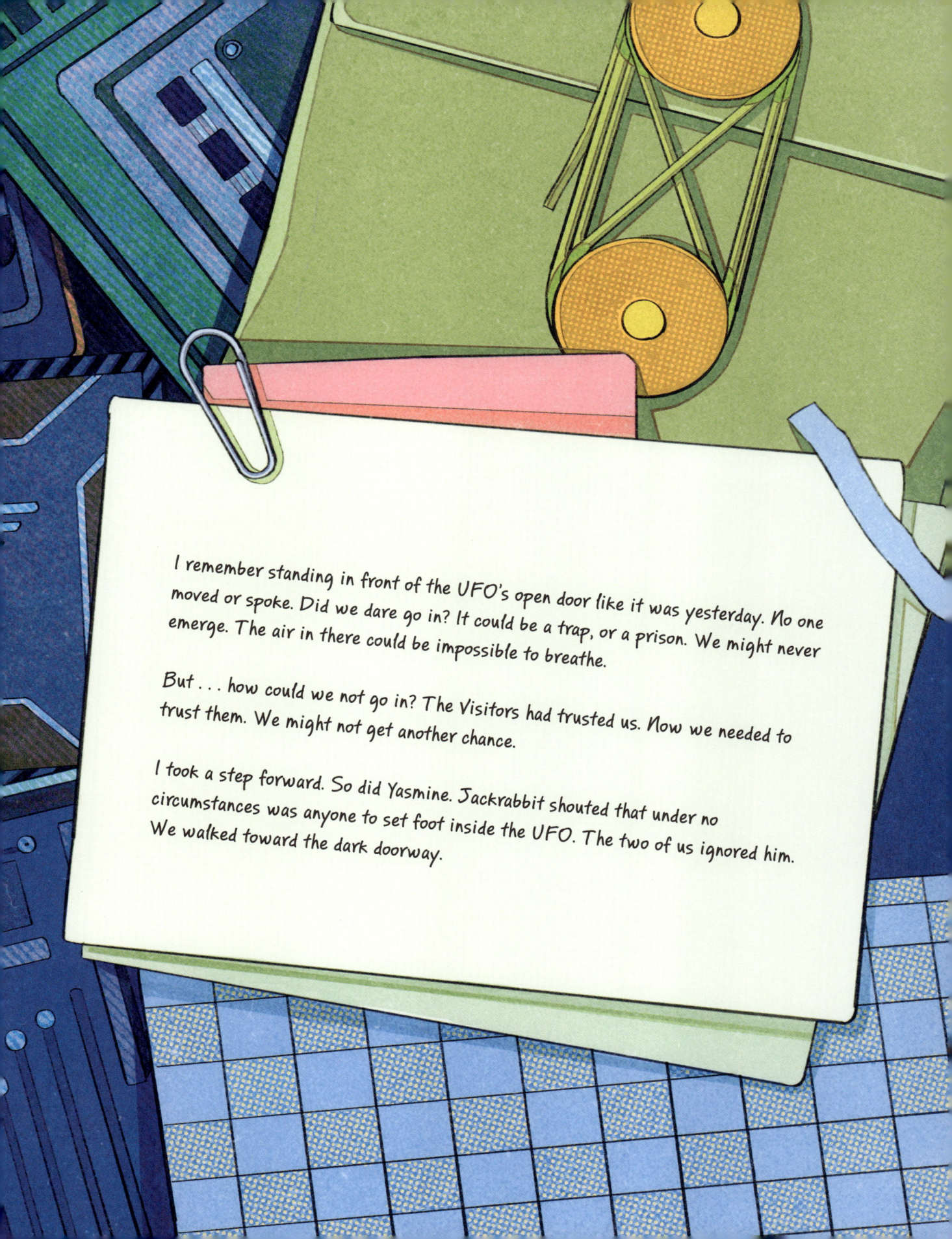

I remember standing in front of the UFO's open door like it was yesterday. No one moved or spoke. Did we dare go in? It could be a trap, or a prison. We might never emerge. The air in there could be impossible to breathe.

But . . . how could we not go in? The Visitors had trusted us. Now we needed to trust them. We might not get another chance.

I took a step forward. So did Yasmine. Jackrabbit shouted that under no circumstances was anyone to set foot inside the UFO. The two of us ignored him. We walked toward the dark doorway.

Audio recording. July 21, 2033, 10:05 PM

Polaris: Wow . . . This is one small step for a person and a giant leap for all of humankind. We are inside the UFO. We are breathing easily.

Yasmine: Our hazmat suits and masks should prevent contamination. We gave two bottles of water to the BugBots. We can't see where they took them. It's dark in here.

Polaris: This is a huge space. We see and hear a lot of unusual machinery.

Yasmine: The BugBots are displaying something . . .

Polaris: What does it mean?

Yasmine: They made something for us.

[Whirring and clinking sounds]

Polaris: What is this? Ask them what it is.

[Voice from outside] HEY! Come out of there, NOW!

Yasmine: We have to go.

Somehow, in the chaos afterward, we didn't tell anyone about the gift we'd received.

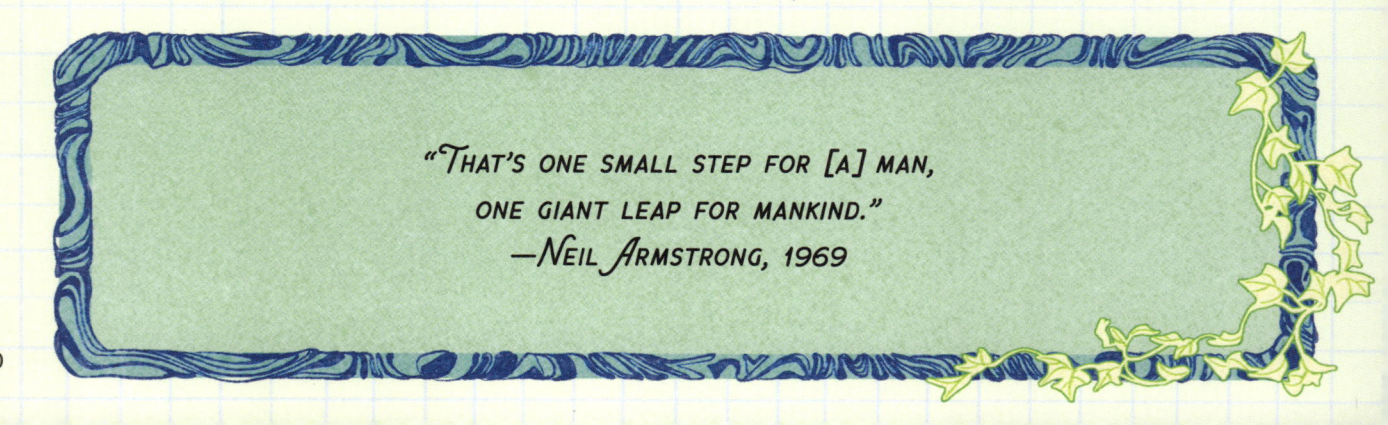

"THAT'S ONE SMALL STEP FOR [A] MAN, ONE GIANT LEAP FOR MANKIND."
—NEIL ARMSTRONG, 1969

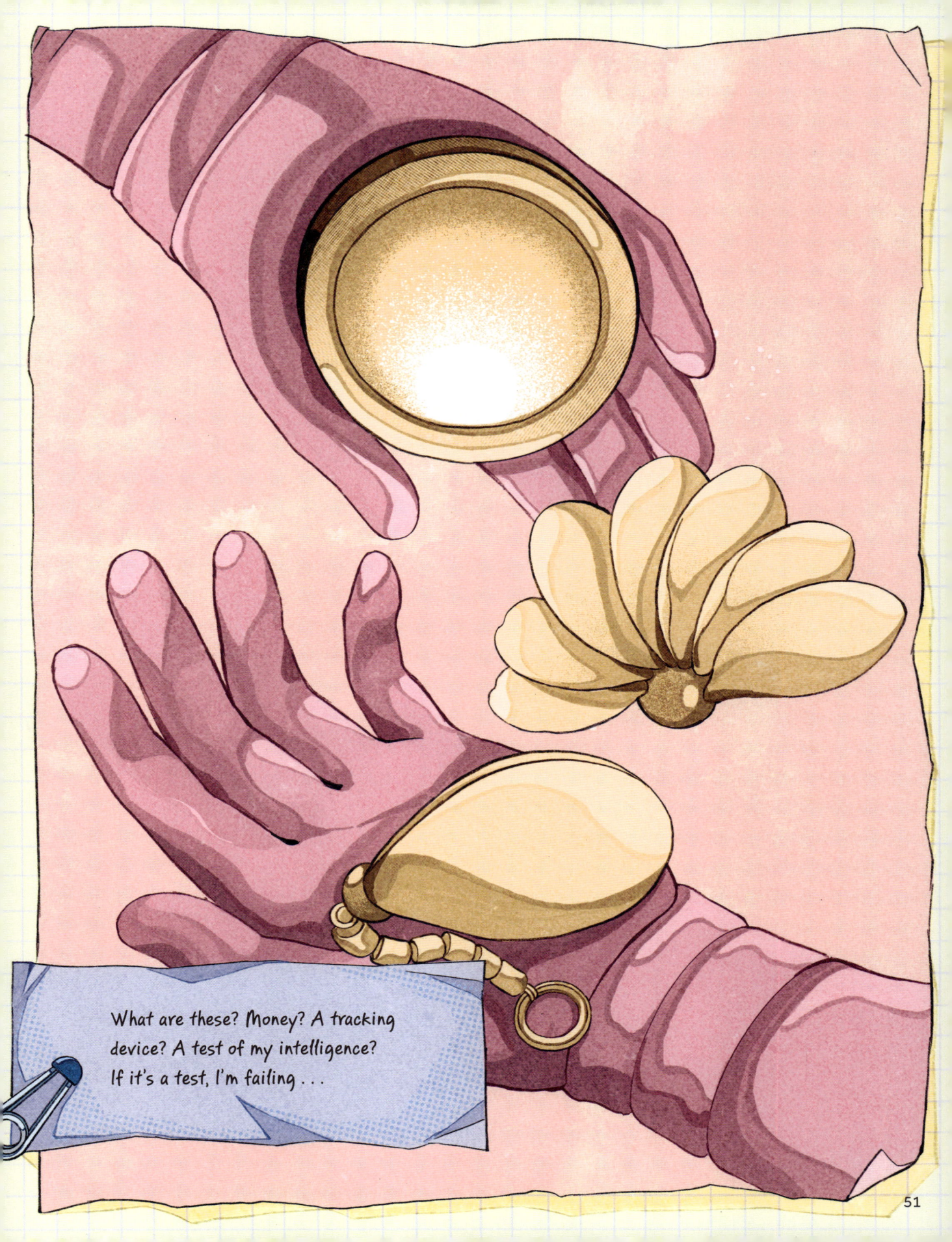

ANOTHER LOOK INSIDE THE UFO

Mission planned for this evening

Investigators will enter the UFO again this evening after nearly a week of controversy.

Last week, two investigators who have not been identified entered the UFO against orders, possibly compromising the entire team's safety. They were asked to undergo medical surveillance in quarantine.

A source familiar with the investigation, who wished to remain anonymous, said they had helped establish communication with the BugBots. "They are excellent investigators and we all hope they can return soon."

UFO Mission, July 27, 2033, 9:00 PM

Team leader: Shane Atwood

Engineer: Carmen Cardoso

Linguist: Henrik Jacobsen

Safety Specialist: Sgt. Toby Brown

Shane: It's 9:07 PM and we are inside the UFO, wearing protective gear and night-vision goggles.

Carmen: There was no airlock. In space, there would be no air in here.

Sgt. Brown: EMF meters detect strong magnetic fields, especially near the walls. Radiation levels abnormal. Not dangerous but unusually high. Multi-gas monitors do not detect any harmful substances in the air.

Carmen: I've deployed two robots to explore further inside.

Shane: That BugBot looks broken. Can we take it to study?

Henrik (displays message): HUMANS TAKE?

BugBot display: YES

Henrik: The BugBots are still communicating.

BugBot display: LARGE MACHINE HOT-HOT-HOT

Carmen: The large machine is the source of radiation. It's probably a reactor. We need a nuclear engineer.

Sgt. Brown: We need to end the mission. Everyone out.

UFO Fusion Reactor Investigation, July 29, 2033, 9:00 PM

Team leader: Shane Atwood

Engineer: Ayan Banerjee

Fusion expert: Maya Liu

Safety Specialist: Sgt. Toby Brown

Maya: Just look at that detector. That thing's spitting out neutrons. It must be a fusion reactor. Amazing!

Sgt. Brown: How does it work?

Maya: Those big coils are magnets. It's using magnetic confinement.

Sgt. Brown: What's that?

Maya: It's like an invisible cage that keeps the plasma inside hot and dense without melting the walls. Inside that sphere, it's like a tiny sun.

Sgt. Brown: Is it dangerous?

Maya: Not from out here. The shielding walls are blocking most of the heat and radiation.

Ayan: We need to study the wall material! It must be something very dense, stable, and pure—perhaps a material unknown on Earth. The magnets are probably made of totally new materials too!

From: Maya Liu
To: UFO Investigation Team
August 3, 2033 at 4:04 PM
Subject: Fusion reactor

Dear team,

From my studies of the samples and measurements taken on board the craft, I conclude that the large machine is indeed a fusion reactor. Remarkably, the Visitors have discovered how to make fusion energy work!

My complete report is attached, but here are the basics. The reactor produces particles called neutrons. These heat up the materials surrounding the reactor. This heat gets converted into power for the ship's computers, engines, and other systems.

The fuel for this fusion reactor is hydrogen. This makes sense as hydrogen is the most plentiful element in the universe. The ship may have tanks of hydrogen somewhere on board.

The reactor also connects to the ship's main thrusters. These are not active now. When in space, they likely drive the ship.

I'd love to return for further study.

Sincerely,

Maya Liu

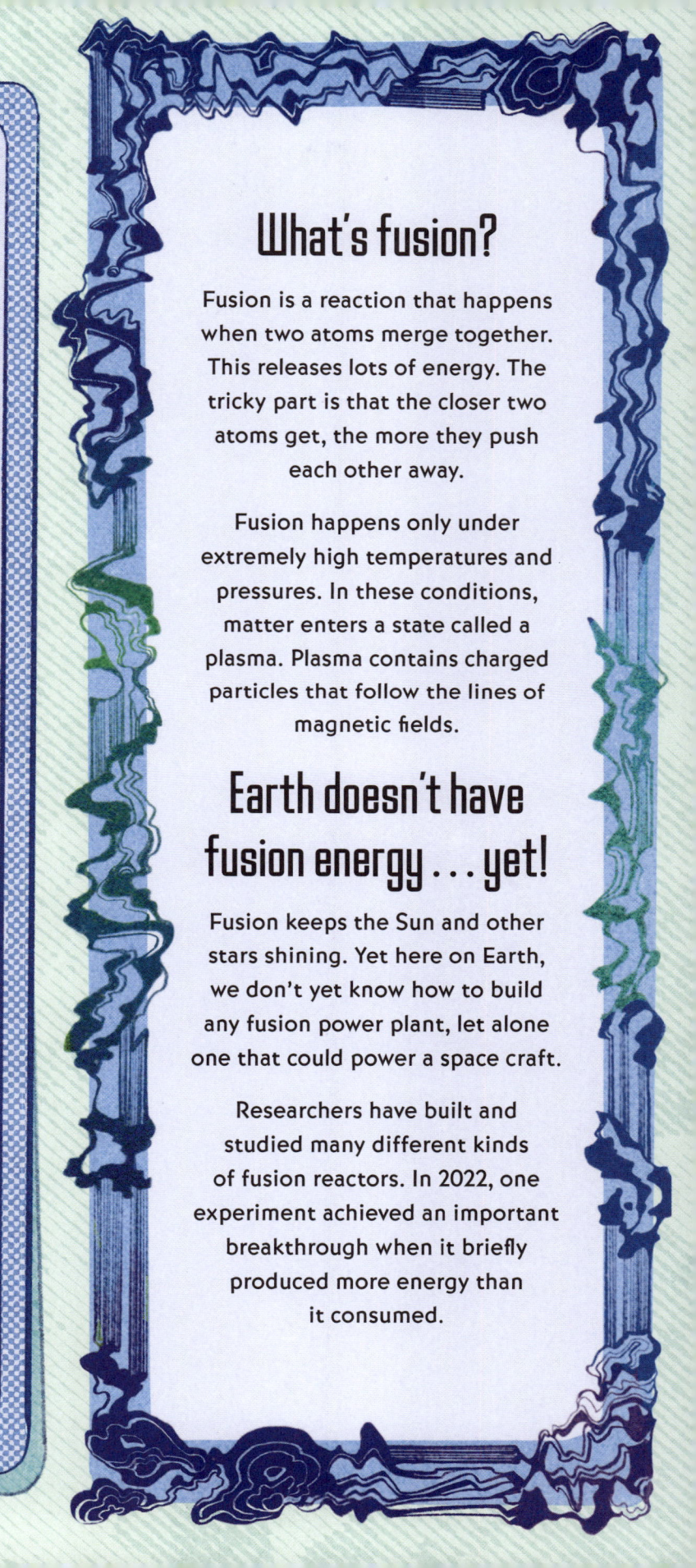

What's fusion?

Fusion is a reaction that happens when two atoms merge together. This releases lots of energy. The tricky part is that the closer two atoms get, the more they push each other away.

Fusion happens only under extremely high temperatures and pressures. In these conditions, matter enters a state called a plasma. Plasma contains charged particles that follow the lines of magnetic fields.

Earth doesn't have fusion energy . . . yet!

Fusion keeps the Sun and other stars shining. Yet here on Earth, we don't yet know how to build any fusion power plant, let alone one that could power a space craft.

Researchers have built and studied many different kinds of fusion reactors. In 2022, one experiment achieved an important breakthrough when it briefly produced more energy than it consumed.

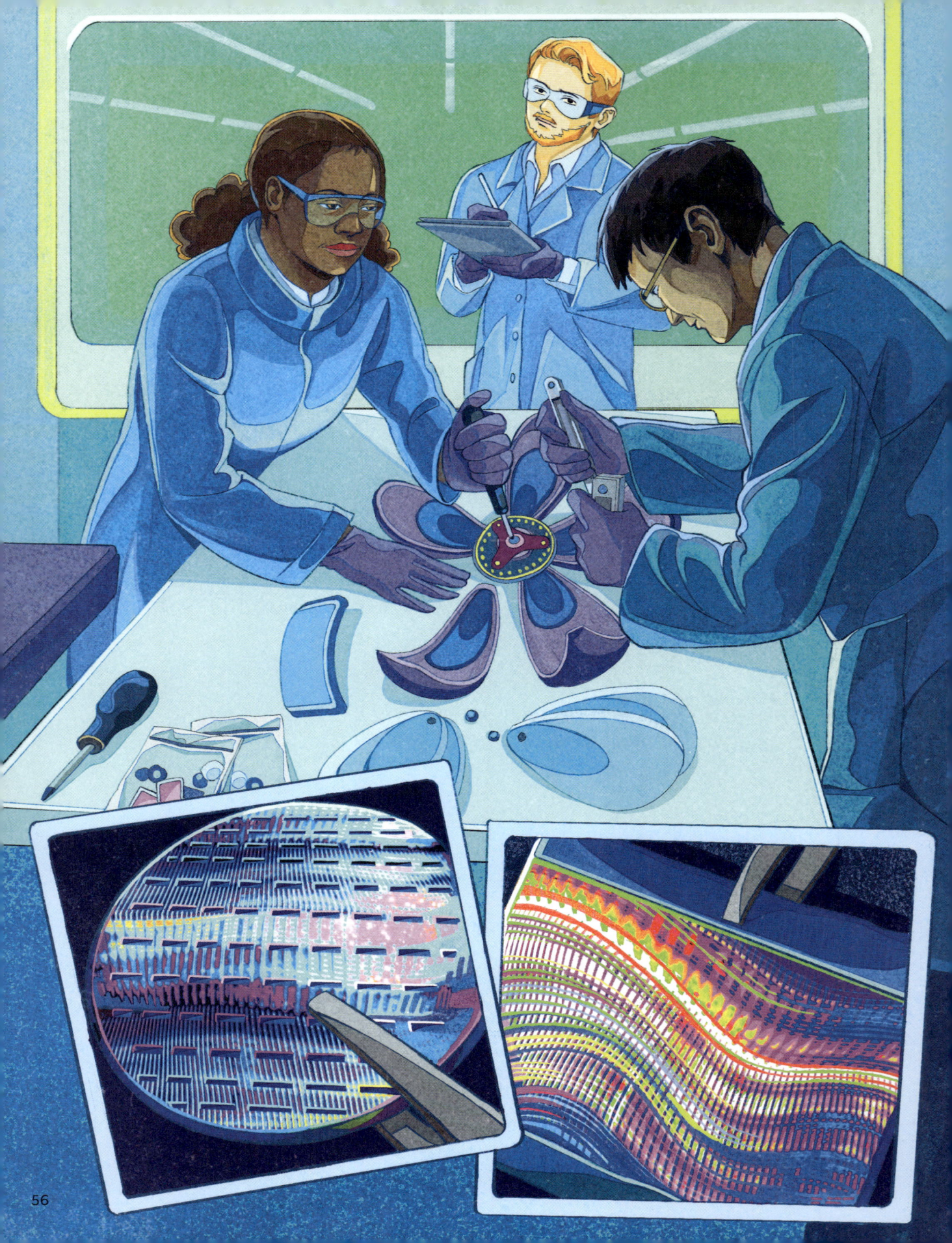

Jayne Stafford [Robotics]: Big news: the broken BugBot contains what seems to be a room-temperature superconducting magnet! We've also detected magnets in the walls of the UFO. These may transfer power wirelessly to the BugBots. **Read the full report.**

Things get even wilder. The Visitors' technology seems to rely on lasers. The small colorful discs on the BugBots and on the UFO are antennae. They send and receive data as laser light. This light then flows through the BugBots' computer chips instead of electricity.

Maya Liu [Engineering]: My group thinks heat from the fusion reactor powers up large lasers on board the UFO. **Link to our research.**

Yasmine Crane [Linguistics]: Exciting news! Go team!

Yasmine and I followed the investigation from quarantine. As engineers studied the Visitors' technology, linguists continued working on the language. And we puzzled over the strange gift. What could it mean?

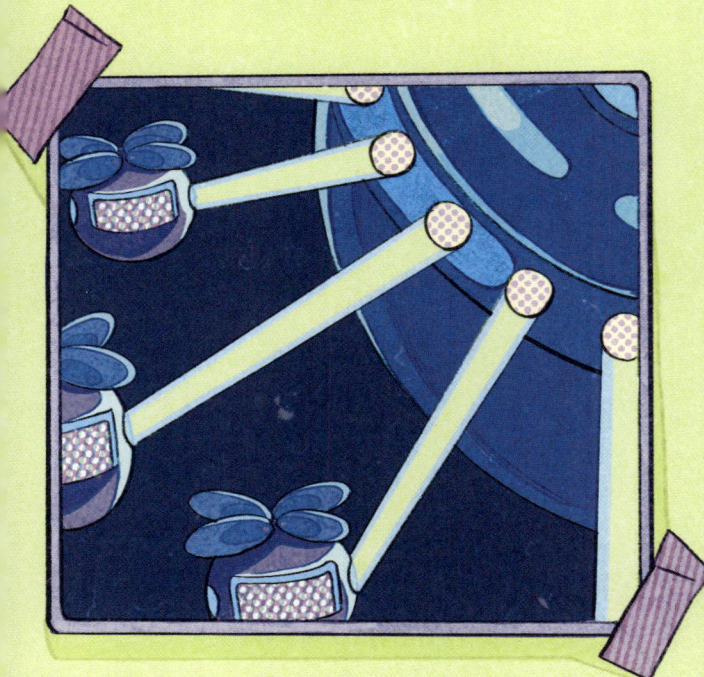

Optical computing

Today's computer chips use electricity to compute. But beams of light travel faster than electricity and without wasting any energy. They can also zip past each other, while electrical signals get mixed up if they cross. High-speed internet cables already use light to send data from place to place. Researchers are working on new technology that would also use light for computing.

Superconducting magnets

When electricity travels through most materials, it loses energy as heat. A superconductor lets electricity through without wasting any energy. Most superconducting materials only work when they are kept extremely cold. A room-temperature superconductor would be a remarkable discovery.

Lasers

Lasers force light into a very narrow beam. This beam can travel a long distance and focus a lot of energy onto a very small area.

Research Proposal:
Project 01875

Summary: One machine in the UFO seems to be for additive manufacturing, more commonly called 3D printing (see circled object in attached image). It appears to be running. We propose to observe this machine over several nights to determine what it is making and why.

Status: APPROVED

Comment: It is indeed very important to learn if the BugBots are building something! Your team will be part of an expedition to take place August 4–5.

Feedstock: several types of metals, glass, and unidentified materials.

Nozzle: this deposits the materials.

Plate: the print sticks to this plate.

3D printing

A 3D printer is a machine that uses a virtual 3D model to construct a real object. In the most popular 3D printers today, a spool of plastic feeds into a nozzle. The nozzle gradually melts the plastic as it moves around, building up an object layer by layer. There are many other kinds of 3D printers that use different methods to build things out of a variety of materials, including glass, metal, and even chocolate!

Report: Project 01875

Update: We observed BugBots 3D-printing parts, recycling scrap materials, and making repairs. The 3D printer takes in multiple materials at once and seems extremely precise. We documented a print of some organic petal-shaped objects.

Recycling machines break down items and reform the materials into feedstock for the 3D printer.

Unknown machine undergoing repair work. Perhaps used for experiments?

Safety and Security Special Notice

August 5, 2033

Missions inside the UFO are on hold until we know the purpose of the machine that the BugBots are repairing.

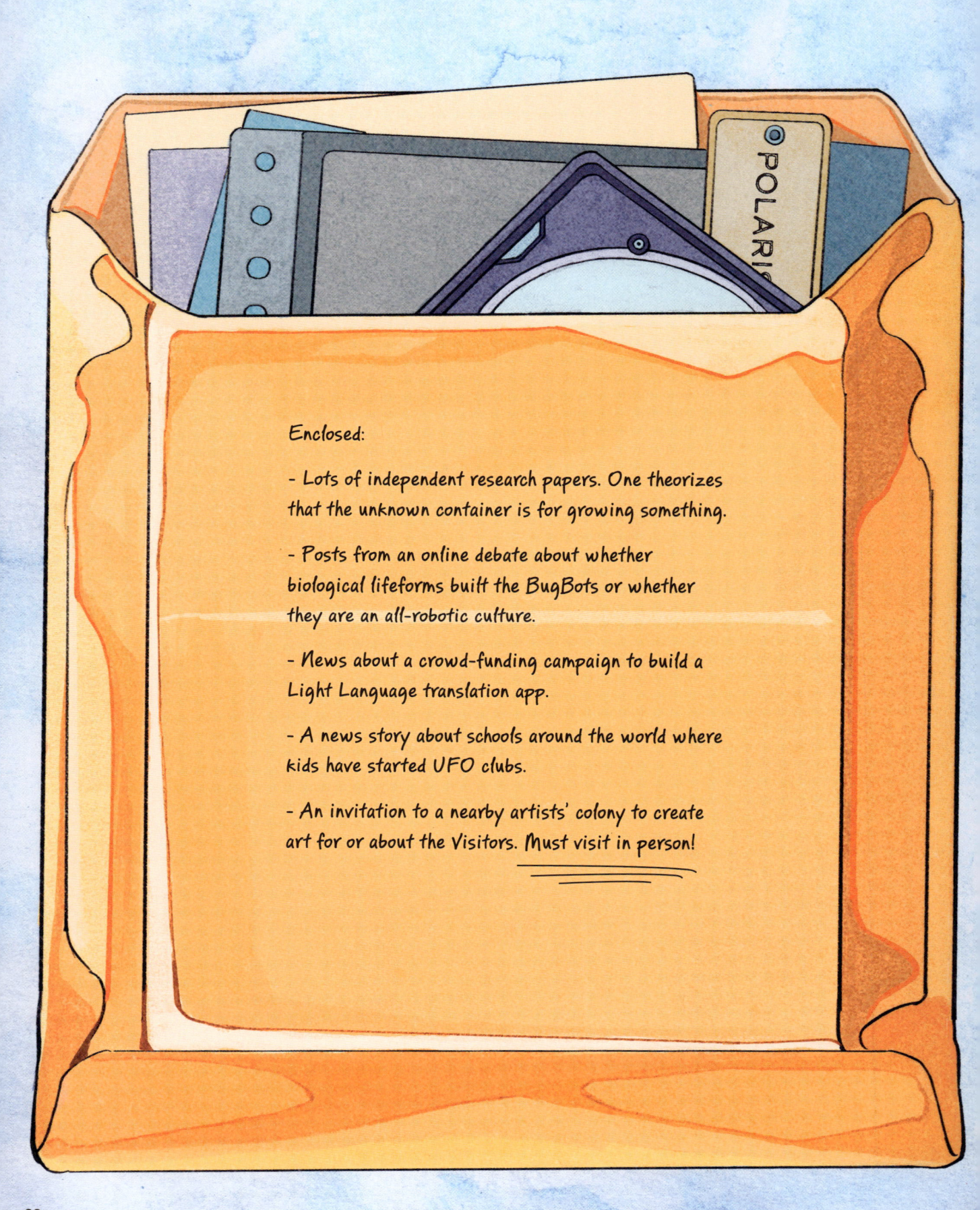

Enclosed:

- Lots of independent research papers. One theorizes that the unknown container is for growing something.

- Posts from an online debate about whether biological lifeforms built the BugBots or whether they are an all-robotic culture.

- News about a crowd-funding campaign to build a Light Language translation app.

- A news story about schools around the world where kids have started UFO clubs.

- An invitation to a nearby artists' colony to create art for or about the Visitors. Must visit in person!

During quarantine, when I wasn't puzzling over the gift from the Visitors, I browsed online discussions about the UFO. Amid the conspiracies and myths, I found a wealth of inspiring ideas: a young couple collecting portraits to share with the BugBots. A vessel for holding water as a gift. After quarantine, Yasmine returned to base camp. But I decided to go meet those working to understand the Visitors through story, music, and art.

From: Polaris
To: Yasmine
Subject: It's a BOOK!

August 7, 2033 at 11:29 AM

We've made a breakthrough! The BugBots' gift is a BOOK!

I showed the objects to some artists outside during the day, under the bright sun. That night, I attended a concert. It was completely dark so everyone would be able to see the lights used in the show—DJ Jonathan Shelendewa found a way to project Light Language symbols along with the music! Before the show, Jonathan asked to see the objects again for inspiration.

To our surprise, the round object was glowing! The sunlight must have charged it up. The glow faded from one color to another in a pattern. Jonathan opened the fan-like object and held it beneath the glow. Shapes seemed to move on its surface. Some of these moving shapes are clearly from the Light Language.

We need to read this book. And I say we work on it right here, at this artists' colony.

Polaris

The Journey

The Visitors' gift was unlike any book found on Earth. Yet it clearly served the same purpose. It displayed text in the Light Language as well as pictures outlined in glowing lines that moved as the light changed. To read it, we used AI translation and worked with linguists, scientists, and artists from many backgrounds. The investigators at base camp asked the BugBots for help with tricky words and phrases. We called ourselves Team Open Book. Gradually, we pieced together a remarkable story about the Visitors' world and their journey to reach Earth.

AIR MAIL

JAN

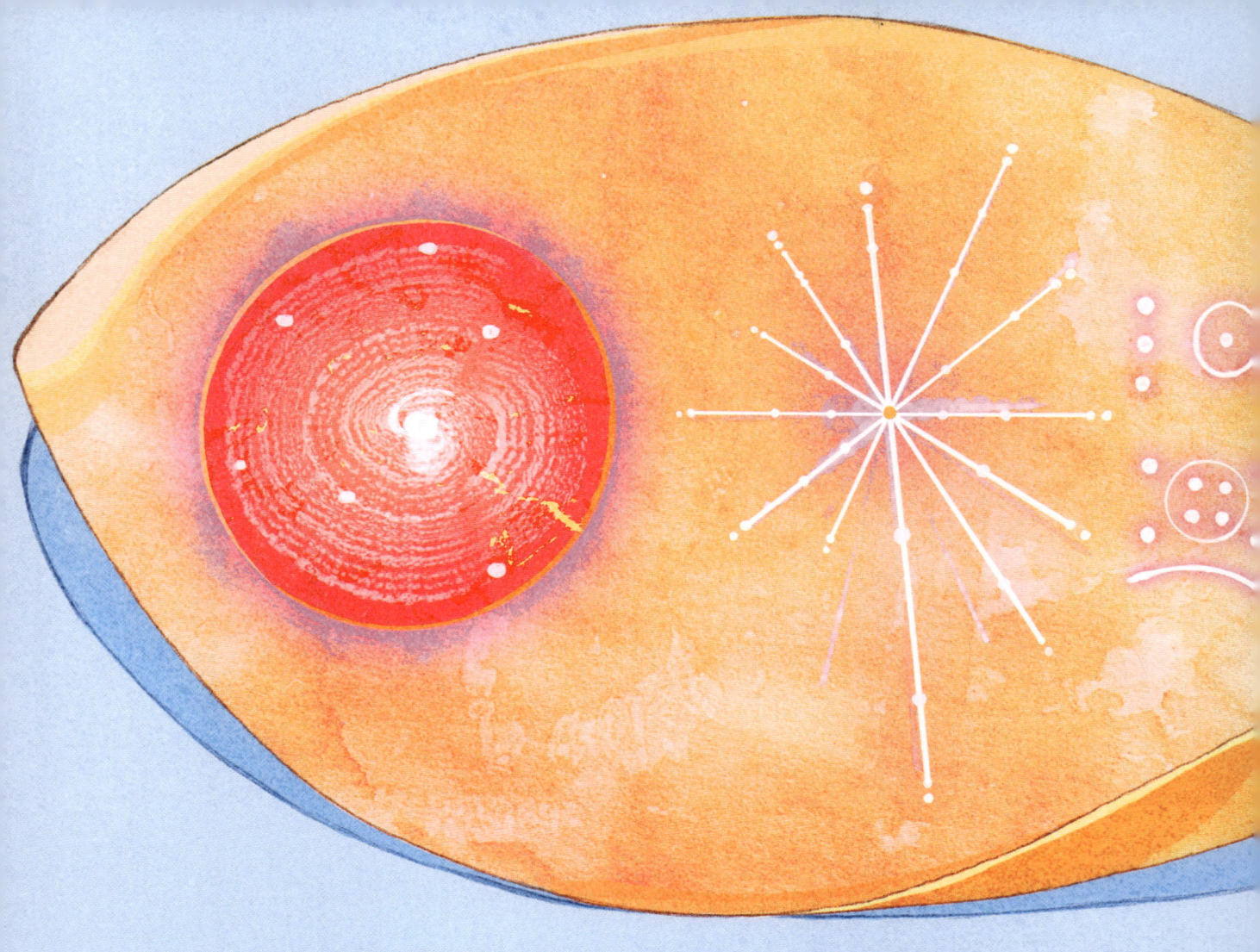

Petal 01 Translation: This is our star. It is old, beautiful.
The map shows our bright flashing-star neighbors.

Team Open Book: The map points to Ross 128!

SnakoRex14: How did you figure it out?

Yong Ling [Astrophysics]: We realized the "flashing-star neighbors" must be pulsars. So we converted the map in the Visitors' book into three dimensions, then found a configuration of pulsars that matches!

Jonathan Shelendewa [Art]: I'll look at the night sky with new eyes tonight. Amazing.

SnakoRex14: We should rename Ross 128 "Old Beautiful."

Yong Ling [Astrophysics]: I think we can make that happen.

Red dwarf stars

Stars come in many different colors and sizes. Very hot stars appear bluish or white. Stars like our sun look yellow. Cooler stars are red. Red dwarfs are cool stars that are also very small. They emit mainly red and infrared light. They can shine for as long as 10 trillion years!

What's a pulsar?

At the end of a very large star's life, it collapses inward. It may form a very dense object called a neutron star. Sometimes, that neutron star spins while blasting out intense beams, sort of like the rotating light on a lighthouse. From afar, the light appears to pulse. The unique rate of this pulse can mark a location in space.

Light years

Most stars you see in the night sky are tens or hundreds of light years away. A light year is the distance light travels in one year. This is a very long way! The Earth is about 93 million miles from the Sun, but it takes light just eight minutes to zip across all that space.

Old Beautiful is a red dwarf star located eleven light years away in the constellation Virgo.

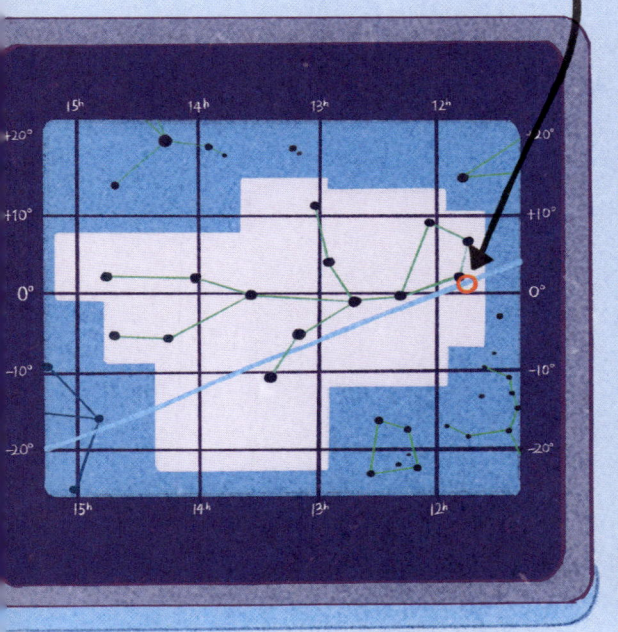

THE VISITORS REVEAL THEIR HOME PLANET!

This morning, Team Open Book released a new translation. Nora Willis, an astrobiologist with the investigation, says this passage likely describes the world where the UFO was built. Did the BugBots build it, or biological beings? And why? "We hope to find out soon," says Willis.

This world has extreme weather and flying predators called "danger eaters." Willis says, "I think our eating demonstration reminded the BugBots of these threatening creatures."

The phrases "near-star" and "far-star" suggest that this planet has an eccentric orbit, one that carries it closer and farther from its star, bringing extreme temperature changes. Astronomers say that days and nights on this planet likely stretch as long as four or five days on Earth.

Another planet in the same star system, Ross 128 b, was discovered over a decade ago. The Visitors' planet was previously unknown to science, and has yet to be named.

The Visitors made this abstract depiction of their planet and labeled it "This is our world."

Ross 128 b

Discovered in 2017, Ross 128 b is an exoplanet: a planet circling a star other than our sun. It orbits close to its star in a region called the habitable zone, where it is the right temperature for liquid water. However, no one knows if water or life exists here. Ross 128 b is likely to be tidally locked, with one side in permanent day and the other side in permanent night. A year on Ross 128 b, or one complete orbit around its star, is equal to about ten Earth-days.

Petal 02 Translation: This is our world. Near-star nights bring city-building and story-sharing. Near-star days bring seas full with water, and skies full with storms and danger-eaters. Far-star times bring frozen-ice-seas.

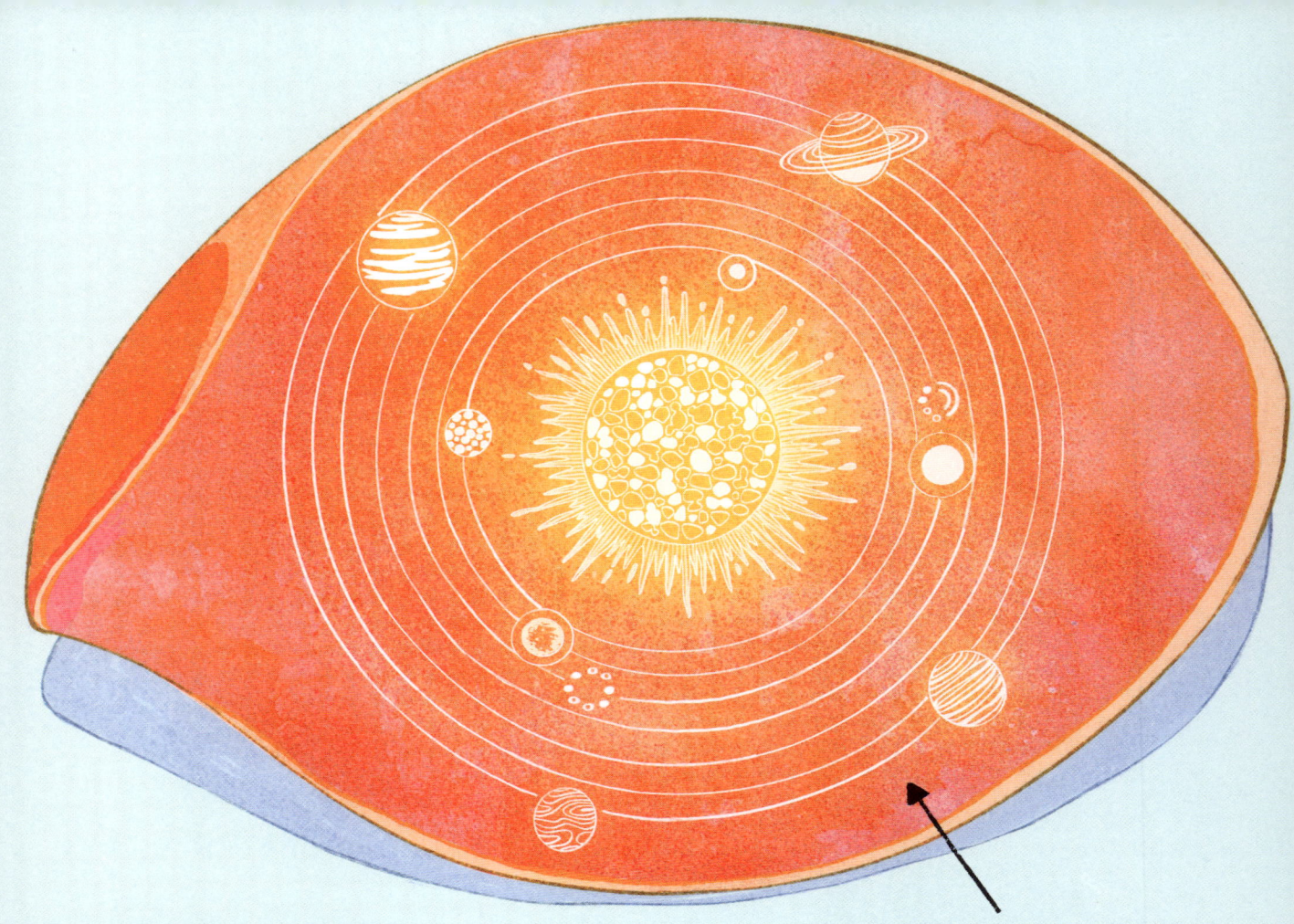

Petal 03 Translation: Each sea is one of many. Each world is one of many. Our telescopes find a young yellow star with many planets. Two may have water. We hear radio calls.

The Visitors discovered Earth from afar. This diagram they drew represents our solar system.

OneSkye Stream Transcript, August 16, 2033

It's OneSkye with your daily UFO news update. Bruh, there's so much hype and nonsense out there right now. Someone I knew in high school spent thousands of dollars on this memento from the landing site, and I was like, I dunno if I should tell them it's probably fake?

So the landing site—that place is on total lockdown. People on the tours have been trying to sneak inside the UFO—more power to them—and the police are like, NOPE. Last night one person was hurt and five more arrested. That "book" says the Visitors like story-sharing. So why are they only sending in scientists and soldiers? I say they fire the entire official investigation and hire us. Me and my fans. Who's with me?!?

This streamer has a point. We should have brought in more artists and people with unique perspectives right from the beginning.

Team Open Book: How the Visitors Found Earth

Yong Ling [Astrophysics]: I found a paper that lists star systems that could detect Earth by watching it pass in front of the Sun. Ross 128 is on the list! It was lined up properly until about 1,000 years ago. The Visitors probably discovered that Earth exists a long time ago. Have they been traveling here for that entire time?!

44.5K

5200

9555

ADD COMMENT

Exoplanet discovery

Exoplanets are tiny and dim compared to the bright stars they orbit. Astronomers have said that finding one is similar to spotting a moth fluttering near a lighthouse from several miles away. But astronomers can study a star to discover whether it has any planets.

One way they do this is by watching for transits. This is when a planet's orbit carries it in front of its star. Every time this happens, the star's light dims.

Another method looks for the impact of a planet's gravity, which can make a star appear to wobble.

Astronomers have discovered over 5,500 exoplanets. The space telescope TESS, launched in 2018, has helped scientists discover numerous exoplanets.

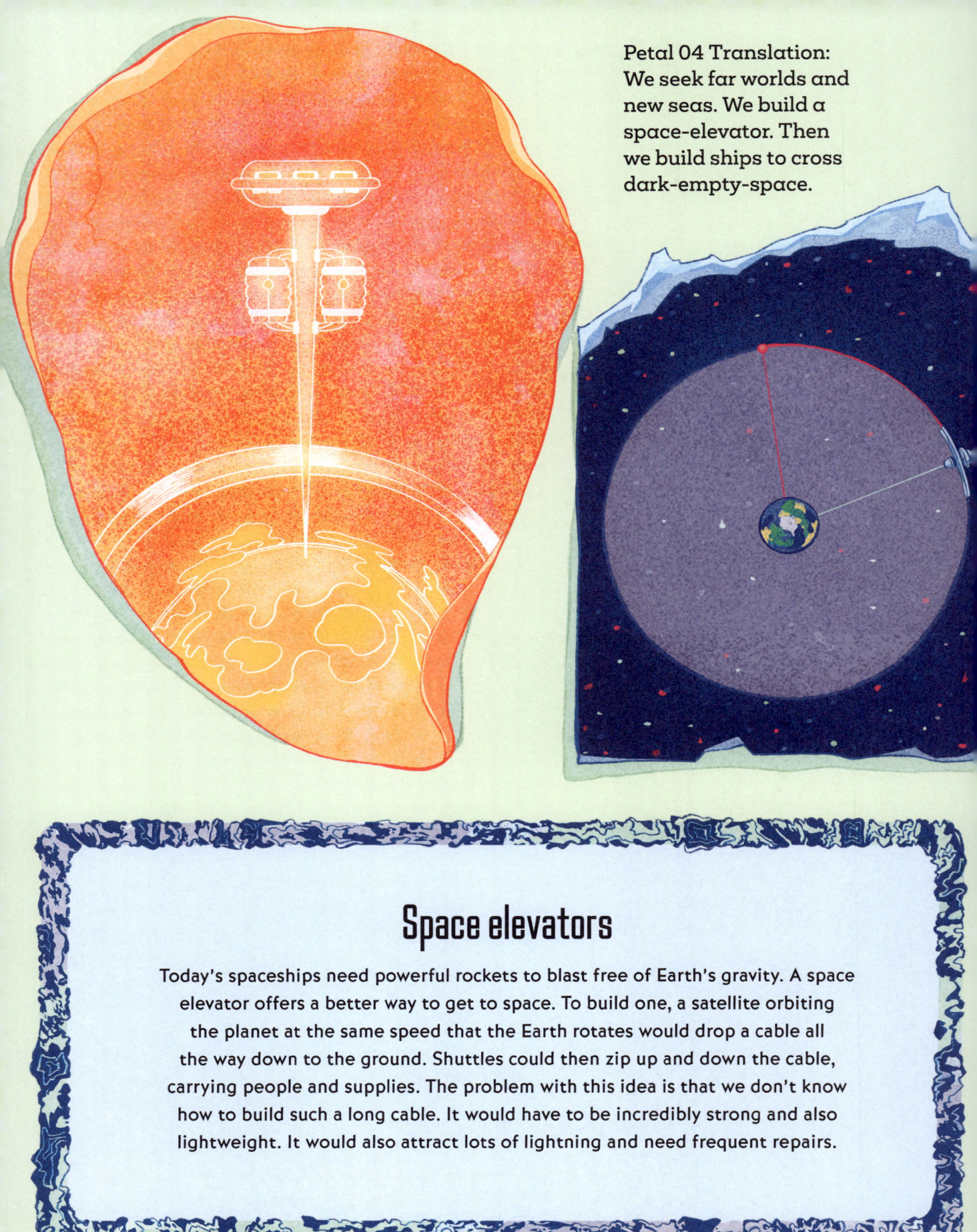

Petal 04 Translation: We seek far worlds and new seas. We build a space-elevator. Then we build ships to cross dark-empty-space.

Space elevators

Today's spaceships need powerful rockets to blast free of Earth's gravity. A space elevator offers a better way to get to space. To build one, a satellite orbiting the planet at the same speed that the Earth rotates would drop a cable all the way down to the ground. Shuttles could then zip up and down the cable, carrying people and supplies. The problem with this idea is that we don't know how to build such a long cable. It would have to be incredibly strong and also lightweight. It would also attract lots of lightning and need frequent repairs.

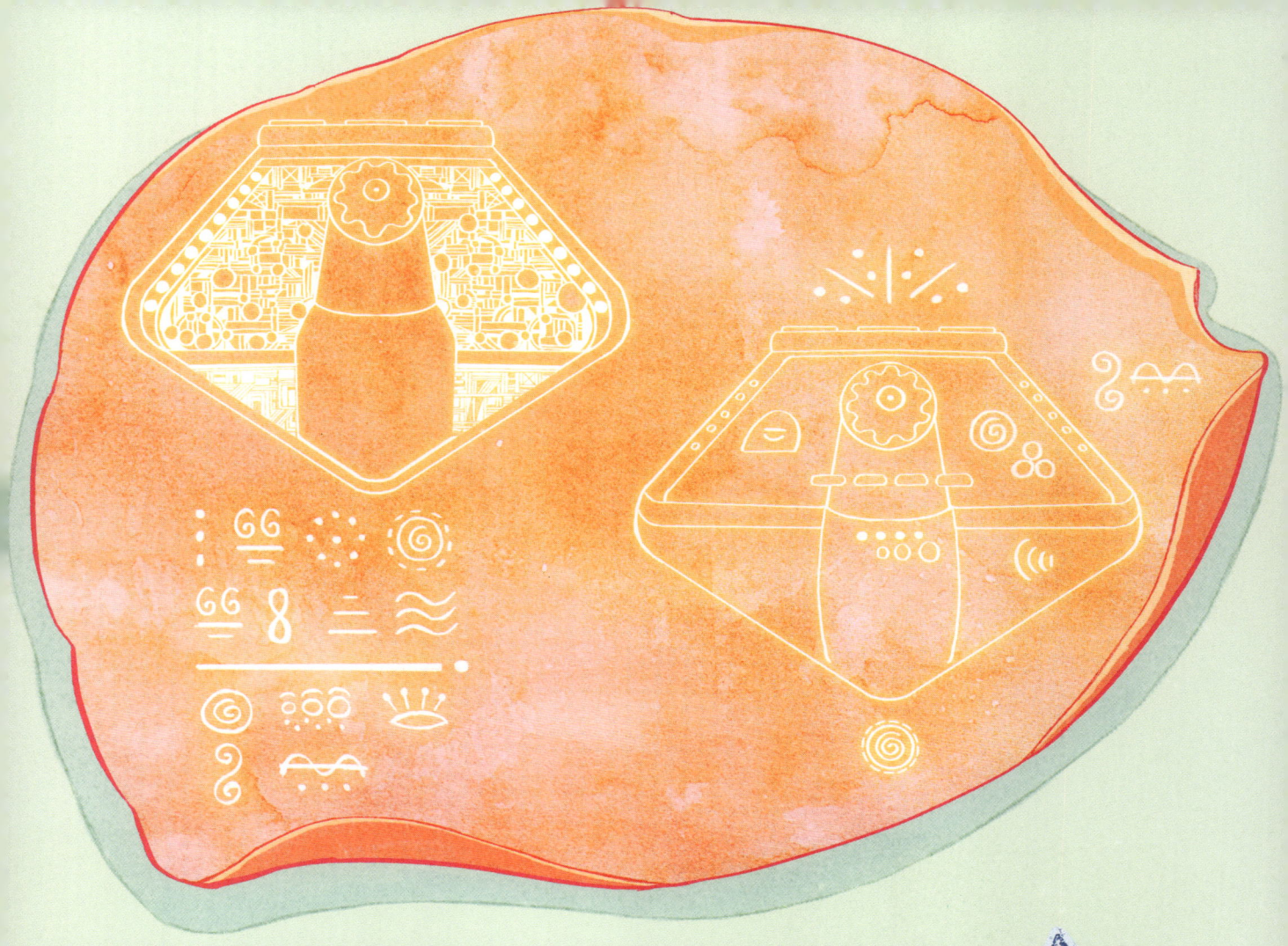

Petal 05 Translation: This is a far-journey ship. It travels to far-worlds and new-seas. Helpers make repairs and call hello. Ƨ dry-wait.

Team Open Book: UFO Diagram

Maya Liu [Engineering]: They labeled the reactor with their word for "star." That's so fitting since it generates energy in the same way a star does.

Yasmine Crane [Linguistics]: The word for "BugBot" actually means something closer to "helper." These robots maintained the spaceship and sent the radio signal. But we don't understand the symbol that looks like a curly backward "S." Any ideas?

Jonathan Shelendewa [Art]: Maybe the seas on their planet have dried up?

OneSkye: I bet they have powerful machines that are activated with water. Maybe we shouldn't have given them water!!??

Team Open Book:
The Interstellar Voyage

Carmen Cardoso [Rocket Science]: The Visitors used a large "mothership" to carry several smaller ships until they'd escaped their star's gravity. So the UFO was already going quite fast when it left the mothership, and it kept accelerating. We think its engines used thrusters that are like nothing we can build. They must have shot out plasma at extreme jet velocities.

Syawla42: I see twelve small ships. Where are the others?

Carmen Cardoso [Rocket Science]: Maybe they went to other planets. Or maybe they didn't make it here. A lot can go wrong on an interstellar voyage.

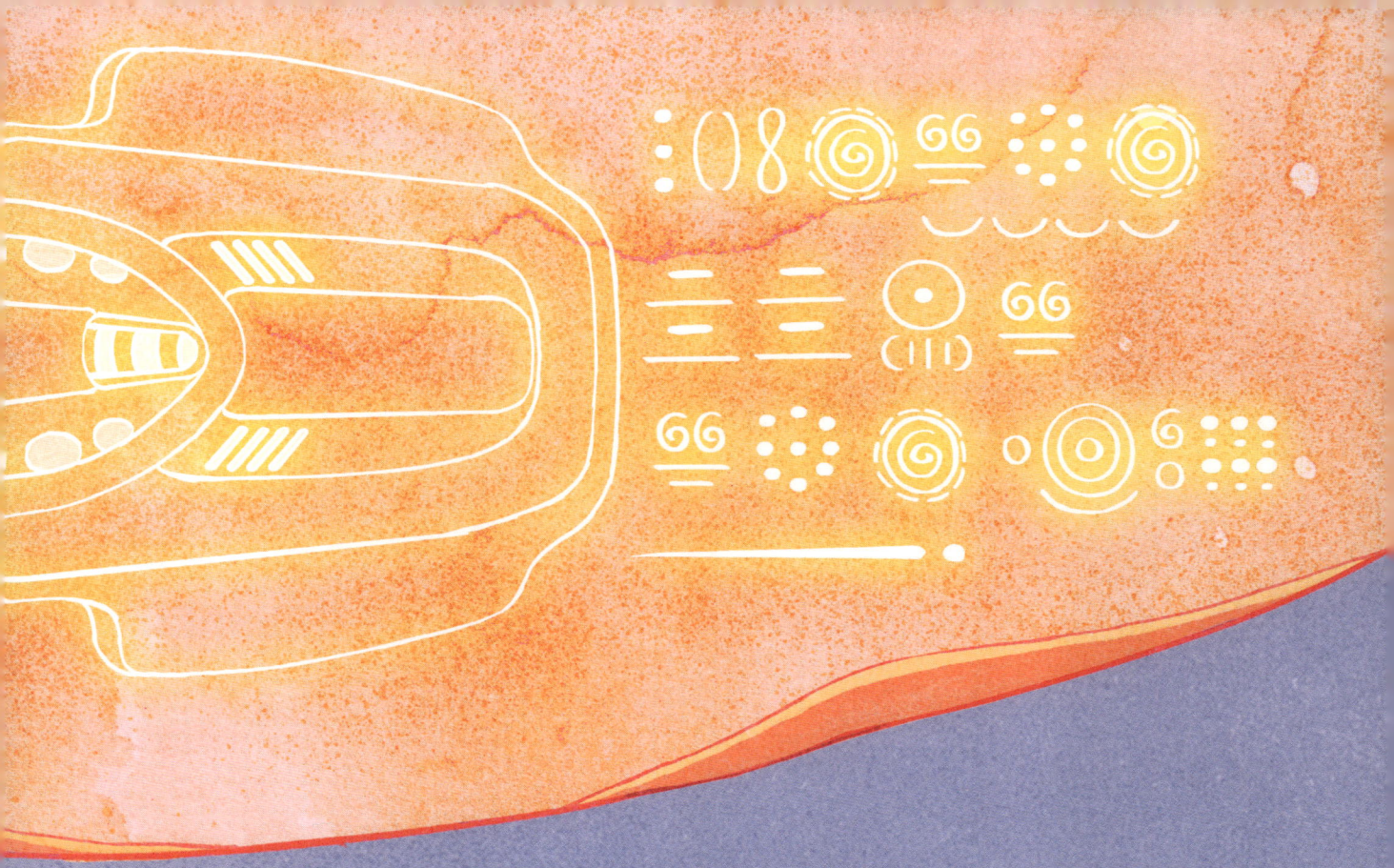

Petal 06 Translation: This near-home-ship carries far-journey-ships, fast-faster away from star-pull. The far-journey ships travel alone through empty-space, long-long-long-time.

Rocket science

Lots of things aren't rocket science, but getting a spaceship from one star system to another definitely is! Rockets fly using propulsion. This is a system that pushes something forward. Today's rockets burn fuel to expel a gas backward, which pushes the rocket forward. Fuel inside a fusion reactor forms a hot plasma. A fusion engine could expel some of this plasma instead of gas. Engineers are currently working to build and test such an engine. Unfortunately, fuel makes a rocket heavy. So the more fuel you store on board, the more fuel you need to move the rocket! No engine is perfectly efficient, and some fuel is always wasted. The fuel conversion rate is the portion of fuel that actually generates thrust.

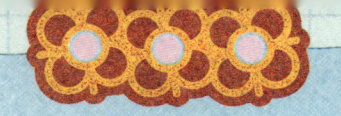

Team Open Book: How long was the UFO's journey?

William Sandoval [Rocket Science]: This has been driving me nuts—I've worked up some simple calculations that might get close to an answer. I'm estimating the ship weighs about 10 tons without counting its fuel. I'm guessing they get about 100 megawatts of power from the fusion reactor, and maybe a 25% fuel conversion rate. They'd end up traveling at a little over 1% of light speed. That's incredible!

Distance: 11 light years

Maximum velocity: 3,950 km/s (2,454 miles per second, or 8.8 million mph)

Journey duration: 1,669 years

Cory Torres [Astronomy]: Your estimate doesn't include the time it took to slow down once the ship got close to Earth, since we know they entered our atmosphere at 12 km/s (27,000 mph). But they still must have spent over 1,000 years traveling here!

Maya Liu [Engineering]: There's no way they have enough fuel to go back.

Was this a one-way trip? Are they planning to stay?

Light speed

The speed of light is 186,282 miles per second. Nothing can travel faster. Even at that incredible speed, it still takes light many years to travel between stars. A spaceship can't realistically travel that fast, though. Why? An object becomes slightly more massive as it speeds up. So the faster it goes, the more energy it takes to speed it up even more. The fastest any human spacecraft has traveled is 119 miles per second (430,000 miles per hour), achieved by the Parker Solar Probe in 2024.

Petal 07 Translation: On Earth, helpers watch for danger-eater-things. ꙅ dry-wait. Wait for water. Wait for story-sharing.

Team Open Book: The last page!

Yasmine Crane [Linguistics]: The final page shows a BugBot off and on. And there's that S-like symbol again, above some unusual abstract drawings. The BugBots don't know how to define this word or explain the drawings in English. These may represent some new technology.

A phone call woke me in the middle of the night. It was Shane Atwood, and he sounded panicked.

Audio recording. August 20, 2033, 3:15 AM

Shane: Sorry to wake you, but this couldn't wait. We need you back here.

Polaris: Huh? Why?

Shane: This is such a mess. A few hours ago, intruders managed to break into the UFO. Jackrabbit sent troops in after them, and there was a skirmish. It was loud and they had bright lights.

Polaris: Oh no . . .

Shane: Yeah. Not good. Afterward, the troops saw BugBots flashing their panic lights and carrying things that looked like dried-up seedpods. One soldier managed to take this picture but then all our electronics stopped working. Now the BugBots are building barriers all around the UFO . . . hello? Are you still there?

Polaris: This is a lot to take in.

Shane: Like I said, we need you.

Polaris: I don't know if I can fix this.

Shane: We need you to try.

CLASSIFIED

TO: Team Open Book

FROM: U.N. Anomaly Committee

The UNAC has voted to place ███████████████ (code name Polaris) in charge of the anomaly investigation, effective immediately.

If the Visitors stop communicating, we will lose our chance at a cultural exchange that could benefit all of humanity—and hopefully benefit their world as well. We believe your team has what it takes to turn things around.

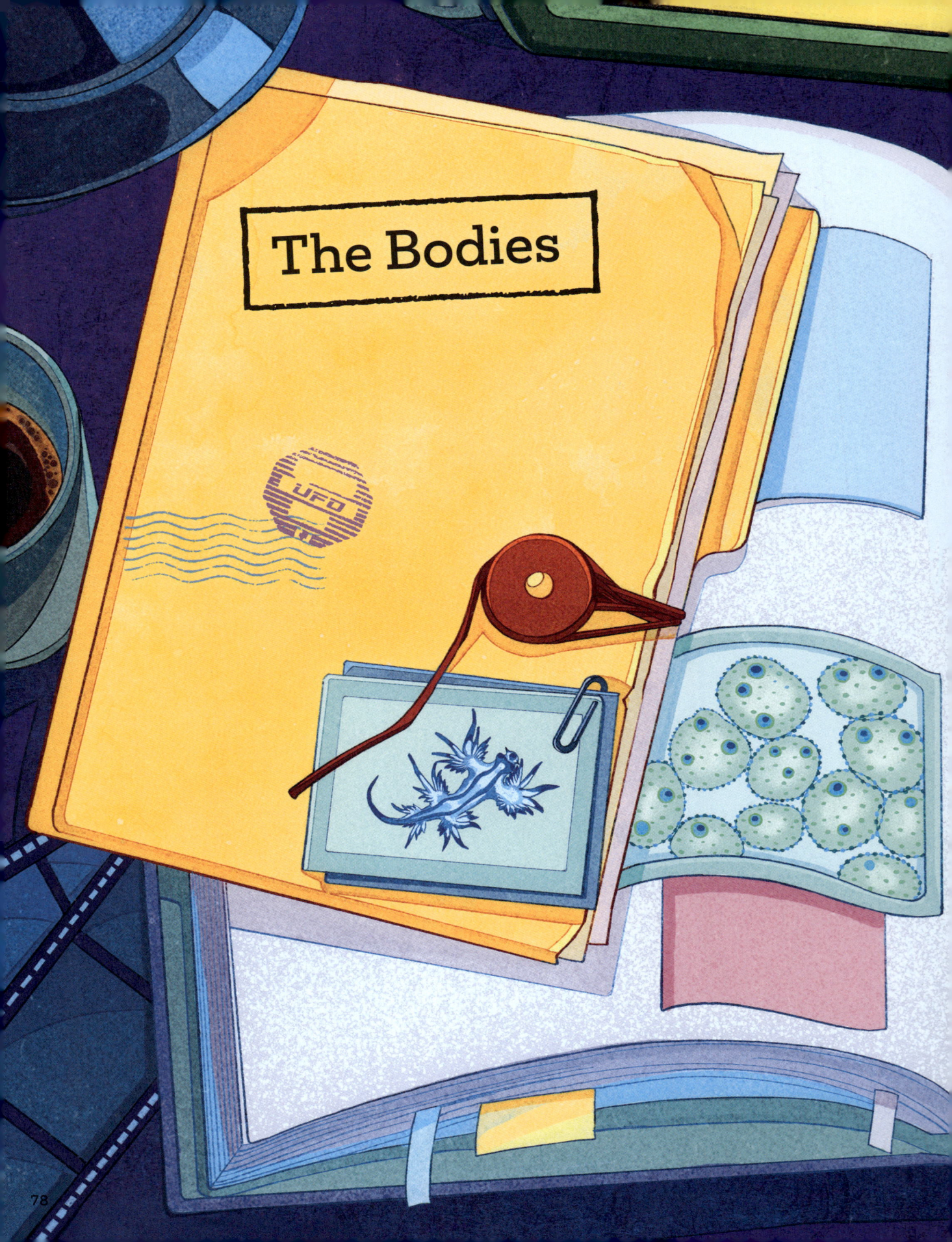

The Bodies

Once I was in charge of the investigation, I wanted to fire Jackrabbit. But the rest of the team talked me out of it. His cautious perspective was still valuable, they said. What kept me awake at night were the seed pods the soldiers saw. Were they dead specimens, like mummies? Or were they somehow alive? Could they be the "dry-waiting" things from the book?

To find out, we had to regain the trust of the BugBots. That wasn't going to be easy. The landing site had descended into chaos. Angry protestors picketed all along the fences. Computer and sensor systems were down or malfunctioning. Jackrabbit's forces patrolled at all hours of the day and night.

We had a plan, though. We made a story of our own to share with the Visitors.

Jonathan played for two nights with no response. Then we invited the protestors to watch. As we mingled and waited, tensions calmed. Even the security team relaxed. Amazingly, the BugBots began taking down their walls. Just when dawn was about to break, the BugBots communicated.

Our Story

You shared a story with us. Now, we share a story with you. This is a story about us, the people of Earth.

Around eight billion of us live on this planet! Many, many other animals and plants live here, too.

People come from many different cultures. We speak different languages and have different beliefs, hopes, and fears. But we try to understand each other and work together.

We can't speak for all the life or all the people on Earth. But we will speak for our small group. Your technology amazes us. Your book amazes us. We have never met visitors from another planet before. We have many questions.

Why did you come here? What can we do to help you feel safe and welcome?

August 25–26, 2033.
The BugBot Exchanges,
Night 74

BugBot display: STORY INTERESTING. 2 WISH MORE STORY-SHARING. BUT NOW DANGER-TIME. EATER-PERSONS BREAK-DOOR, BRING BRIGHT-LIGHT.

Yasmine display: SAFE NOW. EATER-PEOPLE NOT HERE. WHAT IS 2?

BugBot display: PERSONS BRING MANY WATERS. BUGBOTS WAKE 2. PERSONS MEET 2.

Jackrabbit: This is a terrible idea! What if that S-thing is a weapon?

Polaris: And what if we avoid it out of fear, and miss out on something wonderful and important?

The BugBots invited us into the UFO the next night to see the Z. They put water into the vat they'd finished repairing. Then they dropped in the seedpod-like things. Slowly but surely, bodies emerged and uncurled. They were alive!

August 27, 2033

LIVE Press Conference: Alien beings revived!

Shane Atwood: Living beings from another world are here, on board the UFO. We're calling them Blues.

Yasmine Crane: We ask everyone to give the Blues respect and privacy.

Reporter: Why didn't you tell anyone sooner?

Nora Willis: We didn't know they were there. They were dormant and hidden.

Reporter: What if they carry diseases? Or catch our diseases?

Nora Willis: We are wearing hazmat suits to prevent contamination.

Reporter: Why did they come?

Yasmine Crane: All we know is they want to share stories.

Some people find the Blues unsettling, but I think they are stunningly beautiful.

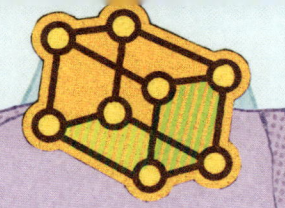

Nora Willis [Astrobiology]: I feel like I'm dreaming. I witnessed the Blues being revived! What I saw looked like a combination of a cocoon hatching and emergence from cryptobiosis.

On Earth, cryptobiosis allows some creatures to withstand extreme cold or a lack of water. "Dry-wait" must be their word for this state.

I have so many questions about these beings and how their bodies work . . . but we can't just take a sample and risk harming them. We have to be patient.

Jalyndai: Cryptobiosis would make space travel so much easier!

Nora Willis [Astrobiology]: So true! In a compartment kept at a very cold temperature, with no oxygen, and with protection from radiation, I think a creature in cryptobiosis could survive a journey of many thousands of years undamaged. It could survive the fall to Earth also.

Cryptobiosis

When a living thing enters cryptobiosis, all of its normal body processes cease. It no longer eats, grows, reproduces, or repairs itself. It's essentially dead, yet can return to life. Some kinds of worms, shrimp, tardigrades, plants, and microbes can enter cryptobiosis. In 2023, researchers managed to bring tiny worms back to life after they'd been in cryptobiosis for 46,000 years!

Tardigrades

Tardigrades are microscopic animals also called water bears. There are 1,500 different species. To survive harsh conditions, many tardigrades can contract into a shriveled ball and enter cryptobiosis. Tardigrades in this state have survived exposures to extreme cold, high pressure, noxious gases, and even a high level of radiation in outer space.

August 27, 2033. 10:03–10:22 PM: Henrik Jacobsen and Nora Willis ask the BugBots for a sample from the Blues.

Henrik display: WHAT BLUES DO?

BugBot display: SLEEP, DRINK, AND ⌒⌒∿ ⌒∿ ∿∿?

Henrik: WHAT MEAN: ⌒∿ ∿∿?

BugBot: DRINK-LIGHT

Nora display: WHY PETALS FALL?

BugBot: OLD PETALS FALL, NEW PETALS GROW

Nora: PERSONS TAKE ONE OLD PETAL? WE WISH UNDERSTAND BLUES.

BugBot: STORY-SHARING GIVE UNDERSTANDING.

Nora: OLD PETALS SHARE STORIES WHEN PERSONS LOOK CLOSE.

BugBot: YES. TAKE OLD PETAL.

This could mean the Blues use photosynthesis, like plants!

The biochemistry of life

Biochemists study how living things get energy and use it to grow and reproduce. Water makes life on Earth possible because it helps carry out many basic chemical reactions. Carbon is also essential. This element can form millions of different molecules. Alien life could look very different from Earth life, but experts believe its basic biochemistry could be quite similar.

How many times has life begun?

Life arose on Earth about 3.7 billion years ago, but scientists don't know exactly how it began. They suspect life started in a "primordial soup" of warm water filled with molecules. These molecules assembled themselves into structures that could copy themselves. This process should be able to happen on other planets as well, but no one knows how common it might be.

Subject: Cells from another planet!

Hi all,

Big news! Biologists put a fallen petal under the microscope. It is made of cells, just like Earth life.

The Blues are carbon-based lifeforms that depend on water. But these cells are very unusual. They use some chemical building blocks that are entirely different from Earth life.

Also, the air inside their tank is slightly different from Earth air. They probably can't breathe our air for long. Plus, our sunlight would damage their cells, which are used to the very different kind of light from a red dwarf star.

Important takeaways for a press release:

- This is a brand new form of biological life!
- The Blues' bodies are likely too different from ours for diseases to transfer.
- The Blues probably can't survive outside on Earth.

Sincerely,

Shane Atwood

The petals are like leaves!

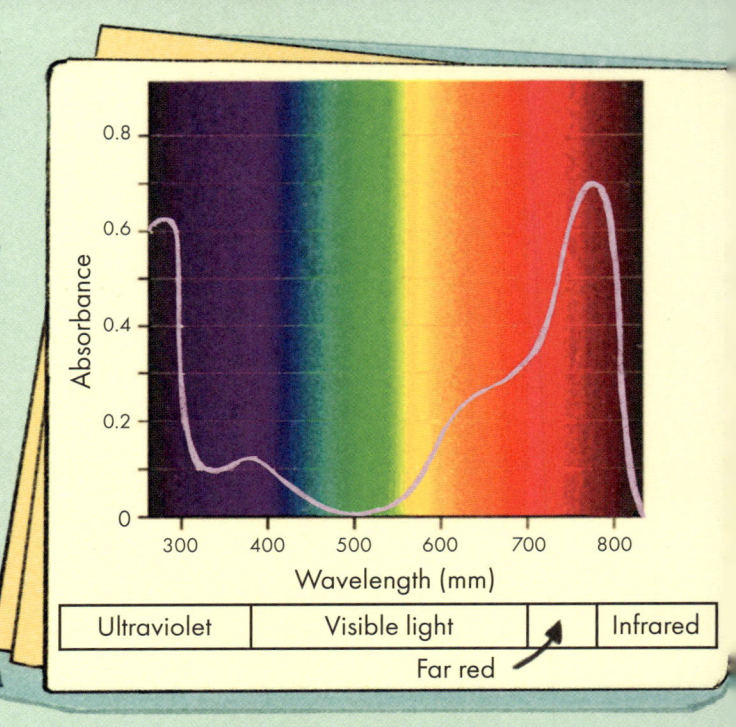

Olanike Bello [Botany]: Hi, my colleague Grace Ibe and I are new here. We've discovered that the Blues use photosynthesis! They take in light in the infrared and far red. That's different from most Earth plants. And it's why they appear blue, not green. **Read our research.**

Absorbance vs Wavelength (mm)

| Ultraviolet | Visible light | | Infrared |

Far red

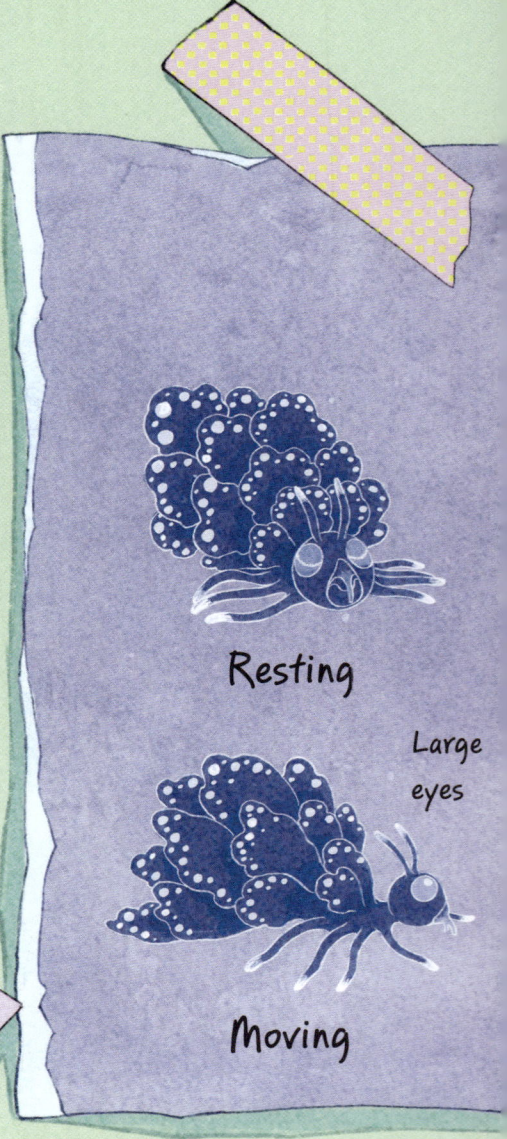

Resting

Large eyes

Moving

Visitors Forum: Plant or animal?

Nora Willis [Astrobiology]: The Blues use photosynthesis like plants. But this wouldn't provide enough energy to fuel movement or a large brain. So they also take in food (similar to algae) using a suction-like mouth. Their tentacles likely function as legs or hands. They have two sets of eyes. We don't know yet what other senses they might use.

SeleneCat101: So, they are a combination of plant and animal—a planimal?

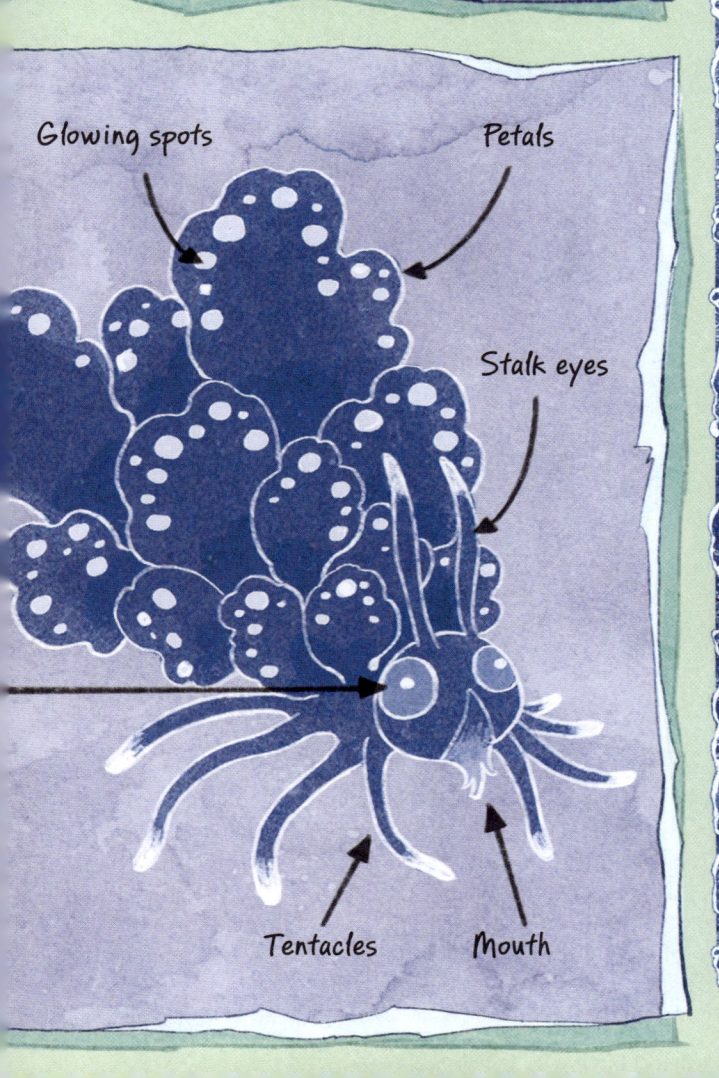

Glowing spots

Petals

Stalk eyes

Tentacles

Mouth

Energy from sunlight

In photosynthesis, a plant uses energy from sunlight to perform a series of chemical reactions. These reactions turn water and carbon dioxide into sugars, which the plant uses to grow. The process also gives off oxygen, which people and animals breathe.

Why are plants green?

Almost all Earth plants use energy from blue and red light. They reflect green light, so that's the color they appear. But plants on other planets might be different colors.

Sea slugs that are part plant

Some sea slugs eat algae. They then reuse the algae machinery that performs photosynthesis in their own cells!

Leaf slug

Lettuce slug

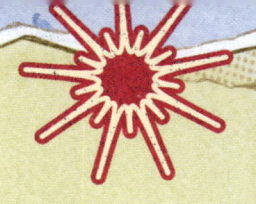

Visitors Forum: The Blues make their own light

Yasmine Crane [Linguistics]: Tonight the glowing spots on the Blues' petals began moving! They are displaying new colors and patterns, too.

Nora Willis [Astrobiology]: The glow is called bioluminescence. The Blues likely evolved this as a form of communication, since they are most active at night.

OneSkye: Do the Blues make any sounds?

Yong Ling [Astrophysics]: They haven't yet. I wonder if the high winds on their planet drown out most sound?

Yasmine Crane [Linguistics]: I think instead of talking, they display the Light Language using their petals.

Evolution

Evolution is a natural process that allows life to adapt to many different environments. When a trait helps a living thing to survive, it is more likely to have babies and pass the helpful trait on to the next generation. Eyes evolved gradually from simple, light-sensitive cells. Some features, such as wings for flight, work so well that they have evolved more than once, in insects, bats, and birds. Scientists predict that any alien life also must evolve. And many of its adaptations will likely resemble ones common on Earth, such as eyes or wings.

Bioluminescence

Many life forms make their own light, from fish and jellies to fireflies and fungi. In the deep ocean, bioluminescence lights up the darkness like fireworks. Some creatures seem to use light as a form of communication.

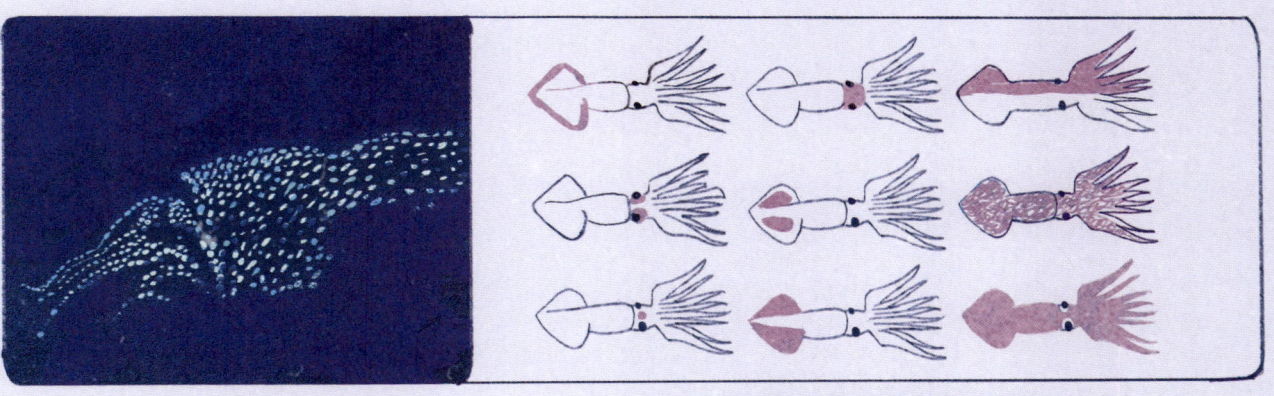

Firefly squid pattern   Humboldt squid patterns

I began working with the United Nations Anomaly Committee to draft new rights and laws, and completely failed to keep up with the flurry of activity among the scientists studying the Blues. For days, I didn't add anything to my files at all. But I finally found some time to pick up this notebook up again.

NewsNow with Special Guest Yasmine Crane

Host: We can't get enough BugBots and Blues! What's the latest?

Yasmine: The Blues are still in a state similar to sleep. But the BugBots say they'll wake up in three Earth-nights, on Friday, September 9.

Host: What if they decide humans are too dangerous, or too delicious?

Yasmine: Well, they can't eat any Earth life because our bodies are too different—they are growing their own food. And we can do away with our masks, gloves, and hazmat suits, too. It seems that all they want to do is share stories.

Host: OK, I'll stop with the doom and gloom. What are you doing to prepare?

Yasmine: We're inviting people from many different cultures to tell their stories.

Visitors' Rights

WORKING DRAFT, September 6, 2033

United Nations Anomaly Committee

1. Right to life

The Visitors (also known as "Blues") are living beings that deserve health, comfort, and security. The robots called "BugBots" also deserve protection from harm.

2. Right to freedom

The Visitors may live according to their choosing, as long as this does not infringe on human rights. They shall not be kept in captivity.

3. Right to equality

The Visitors shall not be subjected to prejudice or discrimination.

4. Right to expression

The Visitors shall be free to express themselves, as long as this does not infringe on human rights.

5. Right to privacy

The Visitors shall not be subjected to unwanted attention.

6. Right to property

The UFO and all items the Visitors brought with them to Earth are hereby considered their property.

7. Right to justice

Any disputes among humans and Visitors shall be settled in a fair and public manner.

Equal rights

All human beings, no matter who they are or where they are born, have certain rights. The United Nations is one group that helps safeguard them. We are all born with the right to life, freedom, and security. We also have the right to freely express our opinions and ideas.

Whales, elephants, birds, and many other creatures also have some level of intelligence or conscious experience. Many laws already protect animals from cruel treatment. But some argue that these laws don't go far enough. Some organizations are seeking to give animals more legally protected rights. Advanced robots may someday deserve rights as well.

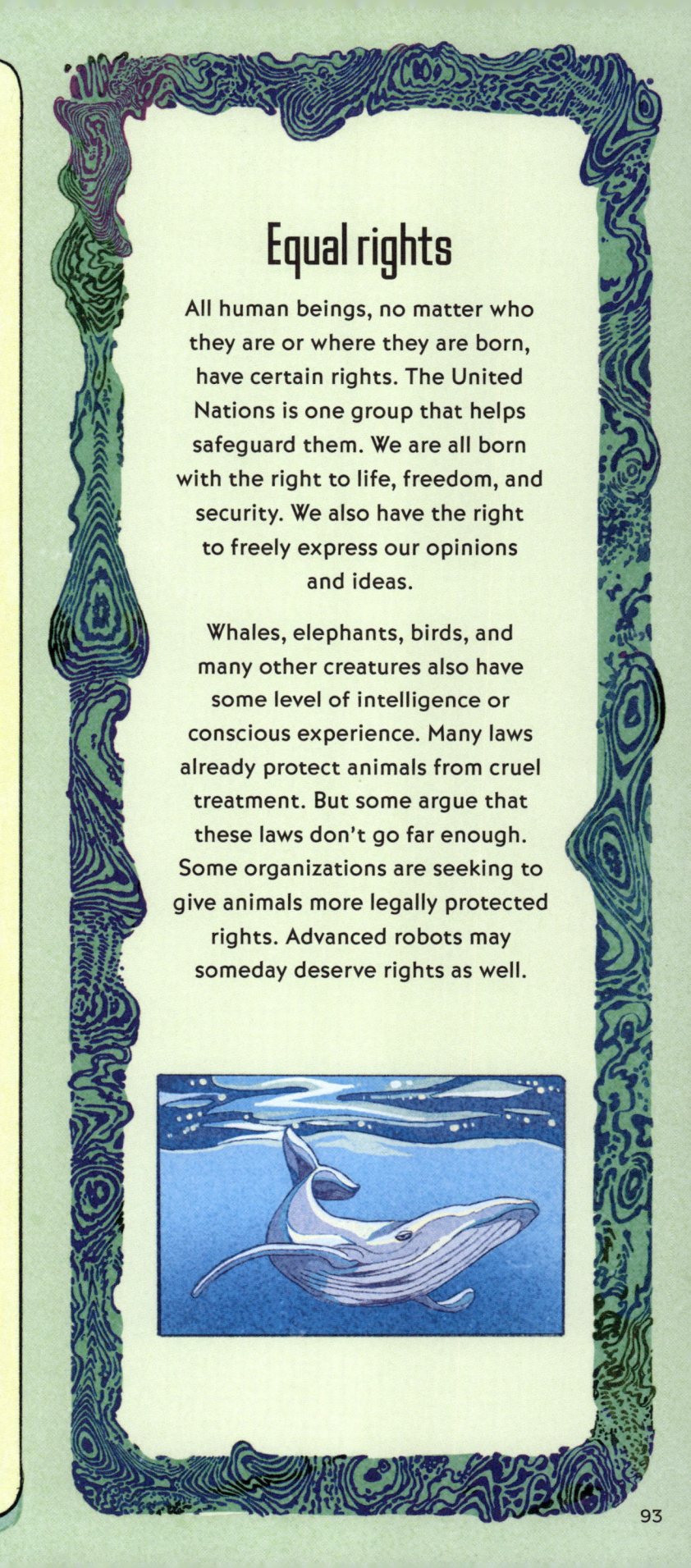

Visitors Among Us

As the day of the Waking approached, a sense of dread began to grow inside me. Humanity's past is filled with examples of fear, hatred, and violence in the face of otherness. And we'd never met anything so different from us as the Visitors. We'd already scared each other several times. Could this visit end with us harming or destroying each other?

I had to hold onto hope that humanity was changing for the better, that I wasn't the only one seeking to look beyond my own narrow perspective. Sometimes, I'd close my eyes and imagine myself as a Blue or even a BugBot, hoping that if I could grasp their point of view, I might treat them as they want to be treated.

But still, I worried. Maybe we should have waited for a better, safer time to wake the Blues.

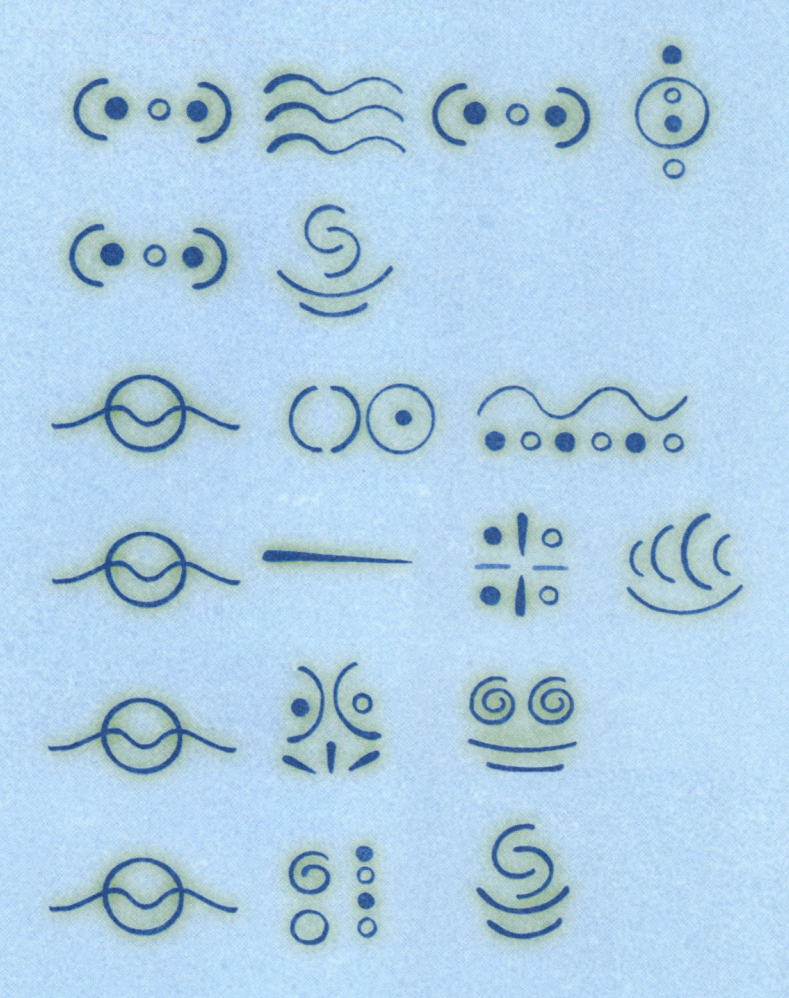

"New seas, new planet

New story-sharing

Wish near-star full-water

Wish no storms calm-winds

Wish danger-eaters far away

Wish long-time story-sharing."

When the Blues woke up, they displayed this poem on their petals. It was the same one the BugBots had greeted us with that first night we saw them lighting up under the stars!

AN OTHERWORLDLY HANDSHAKE

A young girl reaches out and touches a being from another planet. This is a moment the world will remember. Kira Shelendewa, age 11, of Zuni, New Mexico, knew she wasn't supposed to touch anything when she stepped inside the UFO, but as she explained to reporters afterward, "I saw it reaching toward me so I reached back. It felt tickly."

Security personnel stepped in to pull her away, but paused when they saw the Blues' petals brighten with moving symbols. The words meant, "Yes, people come closer."

After this otherworldly handshake, the alien ducked back inside its helmet to breathe. But as others boarded the UFO, the Blues took turns reaching out to touch everyone's finger. (cont'd on p. 6)

Kira's brother, Jonathan Shelendewa, is an artist with Team Open Book. He noted that his sister has always loved nature. "She notices little things that no one else does. She won't let anyone squish ants or spiders," he said.

Kira was one of the forty people selected to share their stories at the event, alongside translations into the Light Language. The Blues also shared a poem that seemed to offer their well-wishes to humanity.

After the story-sharing, the Blues answered several questions, revealing that they plan to stay on Earth.

Tens of millions of people worldwide viewed a livestream of this historic event. Some protests and parties got out of hand. But overall, the response was surprisingly peaceful.

For almost two weeks, my team held regular exchanges with the Blues to learn more about their culture. Artists created images of what life was like on their planet. In order to protect the Visitors, we had to understand them.

Visitors Forum: Seas and storms

Yong Ling [Astrophysics]: The Blues' planet experiences constant wind, intense storms, and extreme tides. Shallow seas, which are essential to the Blues' survival, regularly form and recede. We think the Blues' intelligence likely evolved as an adaptation that helped their social groups work together to find these seas.

Visitors Forum: A multitude of alien life!

Shane Atwood [Policy and Ethics]: The Blues have had advanced technology for far longer than we have. They say many other lifeforms exist on their planet and throughout the galaxy!

To the Blues, our human lives seem quite short and hurried.

Visitors Forum: Volcanic winters

Nora Willis [Astrobiology]: Extreme volcanic activity regularly sends the Blues' planet into a long, dry winter. Entire cities go into cryptobiosis—a "dry-wait"— until conditions improve. Blues can also dry-wait if any resources are scarce, so fighting is rare in their culture.

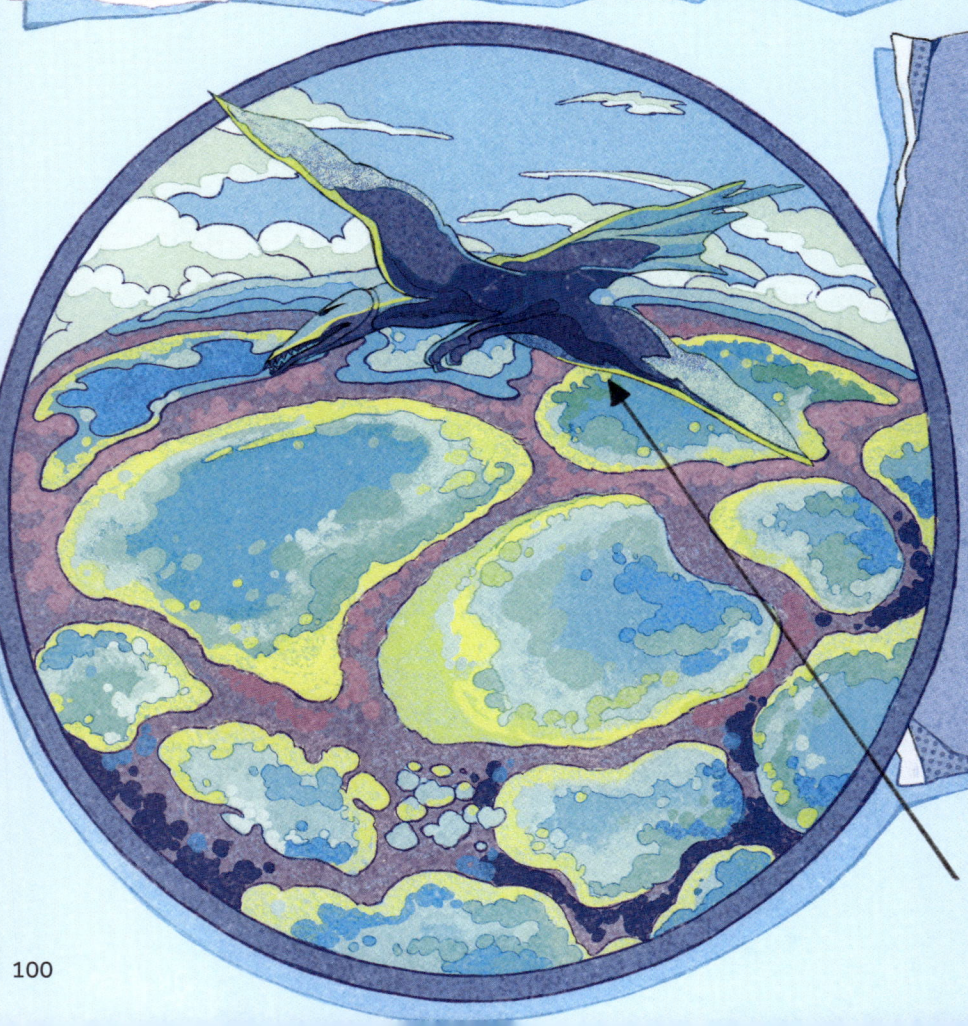

We think this is what a danger-eater looks like as it hunts for Blues.

Visitors Forum: Long lives

Nora Willis [Astrobiology]: Each Blue is both male and female. After a large group spawning, each adult may select one egg to hatch, and they form a deep bond. Blues can live for thousands of Earth years. They don't seem to ever experience old age. Some living things on Earth are similar, including the bristlecone pine tree, several types of turtles, and the quahog clam.

Visitors Forum: Floating cities

Yasmine Crane [Linguistics]: Most Blues live in boat-like floating cities that move from sea to sea. They also fly around using BugBots. Blues sleep and feed at the edge of a city. The middle has dome-shaped buildings where Blues work and socialize. They live in small family groups that are always together.

The fact that people regularly spend time alone seems to confuse the Blues. It just doesn't seem possible to them.

Team Meeting, September 22, 2033

Jackrabbit: Something's happening on board the UFO. The 3D printers have been running day and night, and not just for repairs.

Carmen Cardoso: He's right. The BugBots are clearly modifying themselves.

Jackrabbit: Someone's got to figure out what's going on.

Polaris: Why don't you ask? Come with us.

Jackrabbit: Fine. I will.

Jackrabbit display: WHAT BLUES DOING?

Blue display: BLUES AND PERSONS SHARED STORIES. NOW SEEK ALL EARTH-LIFE STORIES.

Jackrabbit display: BLUES LEAVE UFO?

Blue: YES

Polaris: That's a bad idea.

Jackrabbit: Exactly what I was thinking.

Jackrabbit display: OUTSIDE NOT SAFE.

Blue: BUGBOTS BRING DARKNESS, WATER, AIR.

Polaris display: PERSONS NOT SAFE. SOME PERSONS DANGEROUS.

Yasmine display: WE WILL BRING EARTH-LIFE TO THE UFO.

Blue: NO. PERSONS CAN'T SHARE OTHER-LIFE STORIES. BLUES GO OUTSIDE.

Jackrabbit: I don't like this.

Polaris: They have a right to freedom. We have to let them go.

Blue: GOODBYE PERSONS. HELLO EARTH-LIFE.

"In indigenous ways of knowing, it is understood that each living being has a particular role to play. Every being is endowed with certain gifts, its own intelligence, its own spirit, its own story."

—Robin Wall Kimmerer

The Visitors left to seek other life forms. They are no longer answering our questions, so I suppose our part of their story is done. We will continue to protect the UFO so they have a place to return to if they need it. But it seems so empty now. I feel like a parent whose children have gone out into the world. Except of course the Visitors aren't children—they are far older than me.

Throughout this investigation, I desperately wanted everything to make sense. So I filled this notebook with all the things I learned and imagined. Yet I still don't really understand the BugBots or the Blues. I don't know if I ever will, but I'll keep trying to open my mind enough to include their way of seeing the world.

I'm sharing this personal record in the hopes that it will inspire others to respect the Visitors and give them space. If you see the BugBots and Blues out there, you can approach them, even try to talk to them, but if they ignore you, please leave them alone.

People will continue to study the technology on board the UFO. Hopefully we can use what we learn in a manner that benefits all of humanity. And perhaps someday the Visitors will share the stories they are learning about the rest of the life on this planet. It seems that to them, humans are no more important or interesting than bats or squid or dandelions.

There's a lesson in that, I think. The UFO captured humanity's attention. But there are so many equally amazing things we have yet to discover in our soil, on our mountaintops, and in our oceans. We should all be out there with the Visitors, searching for stories. Are you with me?

Polaris

Sources

This book is a work of fiction, and all of the characters are fictional. However, many actual scientists and engineers contributed their time and expertise during the research for this book. Their feedback helped make the science and technology as plausible as possible.

First Contact

Special thanks to Sofia Sheikh, Chenoa Tremblay, and Kaitlin C. Rasmussen for sharing their expertise in radio astronomy and SETI.

p. 9 Jill Tartar, from the *On Being* with Krista Tippett episode "It Takes a Cosmos to Make a Human," first broadcast February 27, 2020. Reprinted with permission. Hear the full episode at onbeing.org.

p. 10-13 The signals shown here were inspired by a simulation of first contact called "A Sign in Space." Artist Daniela De Paulis worked with the SETI Institute and the European Space Agency (ESA) on the project. An ESA spacecraft sent a message the artist had composed and Earth telescopes received it. See: SETI Institute. "A Sign in Space – Simulating First Contact." YouTube. Streamed live May 24, 2023.

p. 12 The flowchart is based on a real one from the Breakthrough Listen program. See: "BLC1 - Breakthrough Listen's First "Signal of Interest": Verification Flowchart." Berkeley SETI Research Center. Accessed March 27, 2024.

p. 15 "The Drake Equation." SETI Institute. Accessed March 27, 2024.

The Spaceship

Thank you to Nick Gorkavyi and Steven Miller for feedback on meteorites; Alvar Saenz-Otero and Craig Kluever for discussing spaceship design and aerospace engineering; and Kumar Sridharan, Bharat Jalan, and Sreejith Nair for sharing their expertise in materials engineering and nanotechnology.

p. 20 The Stardust return capsule was a real craft. Its journey inspired the shape and trajectory of the UFO. See: NASA Press Kit. "Samples Return to Earth." *Spaceflight Now*, December 30, 2003.

p. 31 BugBots were inspired by real drones and small flying robots, including RoboBee. See: Rob Wood. "RoboBees: Autonomous Flying Microrobots." Wyss Institute, November 5, 2019.

The Language

Thank you to Sheri Wells-Jensen for assisting with the BugBot exchanges and to Gašper Beguš with Project CETI for sharing his work using AI to decipher sperm whale sounds.

p. 35 Anyone is welcome participate in the public art project "A Sign in Space" at https://asignin.space/

p. 37 Hans Freudenthal. *Lincos: Design of a Language for Cosmic Intercourse*. North-Holland Publishing Company. 1960.

p. 37 Yvan Dutil and Stéphane Dumas. "Annotated Cosmic Call Primer." *Smithsonian*, September 26, 2016.

p. 39 For more about GANs, see: Gašper Beguš, et al. "Approaching an unknown communication system by latent space exploration and causal inference." arXiv:2303.10931, March 20, 2023.

p. 39 For more about project CETI, see: Kathryn Hulick. "How artificial intelligence could help us talk to animals." *Science News Explores*, August 17, 2023.

The Technology

Thank you to Shon Mackie for showing me around the MIT Plasma Science and Fusion Center (where magnetic coils for an experimental fusion reactor were under construction!). Thanks also to Saskia Mordijck and Steffi Diem for sharing their expertise in fusion science; Ryan Hamerly and Charles Roques-Carmes for answering questions about optical computing; Aristeidis Karalis for expertise on wireless power; and Keivan Davami for discussing 3D printing.

p. 50 Neil Armstrong was the first person to walk on the moon! A transcript of the event is available here: Eric M. Jones and Ken Glover, editors. "Apollo 11 Lunar Surface Journal." NASA, 1995.

P. 57 Lawrence Livermore National Laboratory. "A shot for the ages: Fusion ignition breakthrough hailed as 'one of the most impressive scientific feats of the 21st century'." December 14, 2022.

The Journey

Special thanks to Jared Squire for answering questions about hypothetical fusion drives and the journey time of the UFO. Thank you to Yutong Shan and Alejandro Suárez Mascareño for discussing exoplanets and red dwarf stars.

p. 69 L. Kaltenegger and J. K. Faherty. "Past, present and future stars that can see Earth as a transiting exoplanet." *Nature*, June 23, 2021.

p. 73 For more on fusion engines, see: Ben Sampson. "Pulsar Fusion to build nuclear fusion-fueled rocket engine." *Aerospace Testing International*, July 11, 2023.

p. 74 Thank you to Jared Squire and Alvar Saenz-Otero for assisting with the rocket science equations.

The Bodies

Thank you to Edith Widder and Sonke Johnsen for sharing their expertise on bioluminescence and to Nadja Møbjerg and Randy Miller for answering questions about tardigrades. Esa Tyystjärvi and Vesa Havurinne shared their research into photosynthesis in sea slugs here on Earth. Arik Kershenbaum and Nancy Y. Kiang answered questions about what alien animals, plants, and environments might be like.

p. 85 "Nematode resurrected from Siberian permafrost laid dormant for 46,000 years." *EurekAlert*, July 27, 2023.

p. 88 For more on why the Blues are blue, see: Nancy Y Kiang. "The Color of Plants on Other Worlds." *Scientific American*, April 1, 2008.

p. 88-91 The Blues' ability to both take in and give off light was inspired by dinoflagellates, a group of phytoplankton that get energy from photosynthesis during the day and glow with bioluminescence at night.

p. 91 For more about how life might evolve on other planets, see: Arik Kershenbaum. *The Zoologist's Guide to the Galaxy: What Animals on Earth Reveal About Aliens— and Ourselves*. Penguin Books, 2021.

p. 91 For more about bioluminescence, see: Edith Widder. *Below the Edge of Darkness: A Memoir of Exploring Light and Life in the Deep Sea*. Penguin Random House, 2021.

p. 91 For more Humboldt squid patterns and what they might mean, see: Kim Fulton-Bennett. "Deciphering the visual language of Humboldt squid." MBARI, March 23, 2020.

p. 92 These rights were inspired by the United Nations' "Universal Declaration of Human Rights" and Animal Humane Society's "The Five Freedoms for Animals."

Visitors Among Us

Thank you to Willi Lempert, Bettina Forget, Kathryn Denning, Jon Lomberg, and John Elliott for discussing humanity's relationship to the idea of intelligent alien life and the possible impacts of an encounter with an alien civilization. Their ideas helped shape this book.

I'm also grateful to students Dexter Greene, Noe Mathew, and Alicia Zheng with the Golden Record 2.0 project. This group is working on a message from humanity to send into space. You can contribute pictures or ideas at https://research.avenues. org/goldenrecord/

p. 103 Excerpt from *Gathering Moss: A Natural and Cultural History of Mosses* by Robin Wall Kimmerer, copyright © 2003. Reprinted with permission of Oregon State University Press.

For my son Seth and his friends.— K.H.

The UFO Files © 2025 Quarto Publishing plc.
Text © 2025 Kathryn Hulick. Illustrations © 2025 Weston Wei.

First published in 2025 by Wide Eyed Editions,
an imprint of The Quarto Group.
100 Cummings Center, Suite 265D, Beverly, MA 01915, USA.
T +1 978-282-9590 **www.Quarto.com**
EEA Representation, WTS Tax d.o.o., Žanova ulica 3, 4000 Kranj, Slovenia.

ISBN 978-0-7112-8845-4
eISBN 978-0-7112-8846-1

The illustrations were created digitally
Set in Baucher Gothic URW, Bernard Gothic URW, PF Reminder, Coronette, and Mokoko

Designer: Sasha Moxon
Editor: Alex Hithersay
Production Controller: Robin Boothroyd
Commissioning Editor: Alex Hithersay
Art Director: Karissa Santos
Publisher: Debbie Foy

Manufactured in Guangdong, China TT042025

9 8 7 6 5 4 3 2 1